BURN

by the same author

SCARS

ff

BURN UP

Anne Bailey

faber and faber
LONDON · BOSTON

First published in 1988
by Faber and Faber Limited
3 Queen Square London WC1N 3AU

Photoset by Parker Typesetting Service Leicester
Printed in Great Britain by
Richard Clay Ltd Bungay Suffolk

British Library Cataloguing in Publication Data

Bailey, Anne
Burn up.
I. Title
823'.914[F] PR6052.A318/

ISBN 0-571-15005-5

To Dad,
Because we made it through

Chapter 1

'We don't want to go to no vicar's house,' Sheena screamed at Micky. Losing her crust.

'He's not just a vicar, he's your uncle and he's offered you both a home.' Micky sat on a wooden box. He was twenty-six, Micky. The brother of Sheena and me. The hero of Sheena and me. 'You haven't got anywhere else to go, right?'

'We can go with you,' I said, hopefully. Knowing what Micky's answer would be.

'You can't come with me.'

Because he was always on the move, Micky. He did so many jobs, see. He had to stay on the move to keep away from the coppers.

'OK, we can't come with you. But we're not kids, you know, we are seventeen. We could go on the road.'

'I don't want to go on the road.'

'Hell, Micky.' Sheena spat.

I spat too.

'I've been on the road. I know what it's like. I don't want you two going on the road. You've got the chance of a good home. I want you to take it.'

'What's got into you, man?' Sheena leant against the wall and slid down it until she was sitting.

'I've just seen my father get put down for life, that's what's wrong with me. Charged with murder.' Micky strode across to Sheena. Yelling so that the veins on his neck were sticking out. 'That's what's wrong with me. Murder, got that? Or don't it mean nothing to you?'

'Oh, he's turned chicken, has he?' Sheena mumbled.

But I heard what she said, and so did Micky. He hauled her to her feet and thumped her round the face. He kept doing it until she yelled out an apology to him. And then she was just lying in a ball on the floor.

'Tina.'

'Yeah?' I stood up. Quickly. Micky was sweating, you know. So much effort he'd put into doing over Sheena.

'Go upstairs and get yer cases. Put them in me car later. Then you can both follow me on yer bikes. I'll be ten minutes. I'm just going to buy some fags.'

'OK.'

And with that Micky was gone. I went upstairs. You know, it was strange seeing the house all bare. With no carpets or nothing. Eerie in a way.

There were four cases upstairs. Belonging to me and Sheena. That was all we had out of the whole house. Mum had taken the rest. She'd buggered off to Manchester, see, with another fella. She said she didn't want any more to do with Sheen and me.

I lugged the cases downstairs and then went to the loo. When I went back into what had been our lounge Sheena was sitting on the box Micky had been sitting on. Her face was all red and puffy.

'We got to go,' I said to her.

'Yeah, we got to go,' she hissed.

'At least it's somewhere to stay.'

'With a poxy bloody vicar!'

I shrugged.

'*He* wouldn't live with a poxy bloody vicar.'

'We're different, though.'

'We're no different. We come from the same family, don't we?'

'But we got to go.'

'Yeah, OK. I know.' She glared at me. Then chucked a box of fags over.

I picked them up and took one. Went over to her for a light.

'It might not be too bad,' I tried to encourage her. But she didn't answer, so I just sat on the floor, smoking my fag. Waiting for Micky. I s'pose it had come as a slight shock when Micky had suddenly turned round and said he'd found a home for us. You know, I s'pose it hadn't really sunk in with me yet. But Sheena, well, she always lost her cool with things. We were twins but we were different in temperament. I'm pretty cool but Sheena, she can blow at any tiny thing. Just like that she can go. As quick as blowing out a candle.

I heard Micky's car just after I'd stubbed out my fag.

'He's back, Sheen.'

'Yeah.'

'Come on then.'

'You go and do your bit. I'll be along, don't worry.'

I could say nothing more to her. Not when she was in that sort of mood. So I went out to the hall and let Micky in. He winked at me. Gave me a new packet of fags.

'Ta, Micky.'

'Come on then, let's get these in the car.'

It took us a few minutes. And then I was just getting my crash helmet on when Sheen came out. Grudgingly. She took the box of fags Micky gave her grudgingly too. I wished she wasn't in a strop with Micky, though. Because we probably wouldn't be seeing him for months. Not after he'd seen us to our uncle's place. And it wasn't like Sheen, yer know. To be stroppy with Micky. It wasn't like her at all.

'All right? Just keep right on following me, ladies,' Micky shouted, above the roar of our 250 Suzukis. I gave him a thumbs-up. Then he was in his car and was away with a screech of tyres. Sheen was away after him before I could acknowledge her. So I just pushed the bike into first gear, opened the throttle and was away.

Chapter 2

It took thirty minutes, that was all. To get from Brentwood in Essex, where we'd lived, to Lower Radford.

Micky pulled up in front of an ugly old house near a church. Sheen parked behind him and I next to her. She revved her bike a couple of times and then smiled at me. So I did the same. She was OK, then, Sheen. Out of her strop with Micky and me. It was because we'd reached ninety along the motorway. Micky had really put his foot down. So we could open our bikes up. Roaring. It was fantastic. Blew everything away. Made yer feel free. As if you had no cares in the whole wide world. Get lost, world. That's what it made yer feel like. Get lost, world, to hell with yer.

'Wow, that was great, Micky.' Sheen thumped Micky playfully in the stomach.

'Thought you'd like it, darling.'

'That Capri tried to burn yer.'

'What Capri? No chance. No bloody chance.'

'He tried it, though.'

'No one tries me, babe.'

'No one tries and wins,' I put in.

'Micky Rudy, tra-la-la,' Sheen shouted and grabbed hold of my arm so that we did a dance.

'Hell, Sheen,' I yelled, 'moving here don't matter, does it?'

'As long as our name is Rudy, nothing matters,' she assured me.

We shook hands.

'Come on, kids. You get yer cases, then come on. I'll go and knock Howard up.'

'Hey, it's a big house,' Sheen said as we stumbled through the gateway with our cases.

I didn't have time to answer, though, because Micky and this other guy came down the pathway to meet us. This other guy wearing a bleeding dog-collar and all. Brown cotton trousers. That's the first thing I noticed. His brown cotton trousers and dog-collar. I nearly laughed, yer know. Nearly laughed outright. If Micky hadn't been taking it all so seriously I'd have laughed.

'Girls, I want you to meet your Uncle Howard,' Micky said.

'Hello, Uncle Howard,' Sheen practically shouted, taking his outstretched hand. 'Pleased to meet you.'

'Hello, Sheena, is it?'

'Wow, he got it right first time.'

'It's a long time since I've seen you. I had to take a guess at it. And this is Tina?'

I shook his hand. He smiled at me. A real, soft, cushy smile, yer know?

'Anyway, come in, come in.'

We went in, through a kind of greenhouse and then another door to the hallway, where we chucked the cases down.

'Would you like a cup of tea?' he asked Micky.

'No thanks. Not for me. I've really got to be going.'

'All right. I'll just go and put the kettle on anyway, for the girls.'

So the vicar departed and there was just us three left.

'Well, girls,' Micky said. Then he wrapped his arms round me and Sheen. 'I gotta be going.'

'Come and see us, will yer? Don't leave it too long, Micky,' Sheen said.

'Listen, Sheen, Tina. I want you to promise me you'll take this chance. Don't throw it away. That's one thing you can do for me. Do it because I love you and you love me. Do it because this is the chance I always wished I had. He couldn't afford to take me in. But his dad, you know, Mum's stepdad, left him a lot of money. A lot of money, and because of that he's able to support you. He's a good bloke. Straight. Don't hassle him. Please. Your dad's in for murder. I ain't never murdered anybody and he ain't before. He never wanted to murder anybody. It just happened 'cos he never had a chance like you've got.'

'OK, Micky,' Sheen said.

'We'll be OK, Micky,' I added.

'It ain't no fun speech I'm making, yer know?' He ruffled our hair. 'I'm serious. Deadly serious.'

It was weird. Hearing Micky talk that way. He'd never been so serious before.

'Oh well, see you around.' Sheen gave Micky a quick kiss on the cheek. Then she disappeared.

'You heard what I said, Teens,' Micky said.

'Yeah, I heard.'

'Don't forget it, will yer? Please, for my sake. And make sure Sheen don't forget it. And don't let her lead yer on. I know she does. But yer don't have to just stick with her now, yer know. You've got a family now. A family to love yer.'

'OK, Micky.' OK. I s'pose I knew what he was talking about. In a way I did. But it was hard. Hard to understand Micky talking like that. And it made me depressed, sort of. 'OK. But how long will you be away for?'

'It doesn't matter how long I'm going to be away for. Don't worry about me, Tina. Don't try and copy me no more. Anyway, I'll be around.'

He kissed me on the head. And then he was gone. He didn't even say goodbye to Uncle Howard. Just gone he was. So I was left there, surrounded by all the cases. Just standing there in a strange bloody house and feeling all weird.

'All right, Tina? Micky gone?' Uncle Howard smiled at me. He was quite a thin man. Had black, longish hair. He had brown eyes. Which smiled. Pussy eyes, I thought. Pussy eyes.

'Yeah, I'm all right.'

'There's a cup of tea in the kitchen for you.'

'Ta.' I went into the kitchen. It was a large kitchen. With a wooden table in the middle. Plain wooden chairs. Sheen was sitting on one of those chairs. Right happy she looked. Hunched over the table. I didn't feel as happy as her, though. All of a sudden I felt pretty lousy.

'Hey, look here,' Sheen said. Pointing to the daily paper which was on the table. 'Look here, our dad's made front page. Him coming out of court, see? They put a bleeding blanket over his head.'

I looked at the picture.

'Great.'

'Bloody front page stuff. That can't be bad.'

I sat on a chair. Uncle Howard had gone. I pushed my mug of tea across the table. I didn't feel like it then.

'You coming out for a burn up?' I asked her.

'Now?'

'Yeah.'

'No, man. I'm drinking me tea. I'm getting settled in, ain't I? With our Uncle Howard.'

'Sure. OK. See yer later then.'

I grabbed my crash helmet and went out the front door. I zipped up me leather jacket. Yanked open the gate.

My bike roared into the silence. It was good to hear the sound. It felt comforting.

I had no place in particular to go. I just wanted to touch the roads. That was all. Open up. Find that freedom. I turned out on to a main road and overtook a red mini, went under a railway bridge and then I hit a roundabout. After that I opened up. To hell with everything, I thought. I was going. Really going. Just me and Lobby. Just getting out. On and on. On and on we'd go. For ever and ever. Never stopping. Never looking back. Never turning back. Just on, baby, on, I was thinking while I rode.

Chapter 3

I was thinking as I rode back. Of Howard. He's Mum's stepbrother. Mum told me about him once. The last time she'd seen him was when Sheen and me were four. It was a long time ago, because I can't remember him. Anyway, Mum and Dad had a big family row with Howard and with her stepdad. And that was it, baby. With Howard. With our stepgrandad. We never saw them again. Micky used to visit Howard. Especially as he got older. But me and Sheen, we weren't really that interested. You know, we had our own lives to lead. But, this is it. Howard supporting us. Howard, a widower now. Grandad also dead. Huh, what a turnaround. I wondered if Mum knew. I laughed. That would make her boil, us living with Howard. But, hell, I was just kidding myself. She couldn't give a shit about us. Not enough to get boiled about anyway. Oh hell, what's the use of thinking, it just makes you churned up inside. I wished I was Lobby. If I was, I wouldn't have to think. I wouldn't have to think at all.

I twisted my throttle and sped past a white van.

Two hours later I arrived back. It was nearly dark. Eight o'clock. I'd gone on. I'd burnt up the roads. I'd felt the heart of Lobby pulsating beneath me. I'd felt her power as she took me past all the cars. I'd felt her vibrations and knew that she was mine. And that she'd always be mine and nothing would ever change that.

I rang the front door bell.

Uncle Howard opened the door.

'Hello, Tina,' he said. 'We've left some tea for you.'

'Ta.'

It was on a plate in the kitchen. Chicken sandwiches. A large slice of chocolate cake.

'D'you want a Coke? Because there's one in the fridge.'

'Ta.'

Then he left me. I opened the fridge and found a Coke. I was hungry, so ate my tea. Then I lit a fag, wondering where the hell I could put my ash because there weren't no ashtrays about. So I flicked it in the sink.

Then this boy came in. I'd never seen him in my bleeding life before. He had blond curly hair.

'Hello,' he said.

'Hi.' He was skinny, yer know.

Then he got a Coke out of the fridge and took a glass from the cupboard.

'We're all in the lounge,' he said. 'Sheena too. It's just through by the stairs.'

'OK. Ta.'

I went into the lounge.

'Hello, Tina. Where're you going to sit?' Uncle Howard said. He had an accent. Very slight. Cockney. I'm sure to hell it was cockney.

I sat on a large old-fashioned chair which was in the corner of the room by an old-fashioned-type gramophone. I just sat there, you know, and felt a right bum. I looked for the telly but it wasn't on. Great, I thought. No bleeding telly. What next?

I sighed. Christ, I felt bloody awful. Don't know why. All hot and stuffy and closed in.

'Where did you go to, Tina?'

I jumped. He was speaking to me. The vicar was.

'What?'

'Where did you go for your burn up?'

I looked at Sheen and she winked at me.

'Just on the roads.'

'Burnt up the tar, eh?'

'Yeah.' I couldn't stick it then. Couldn't stick it any longer. So I got up and went out to the kitchen. It was better in the kitchen. Just me and the silence. Well, just me and the buzzing of the fridge. Buzz. Buzz. Buzz. Buzz. Buzz. Buzz.

Then my eyes fell upon the daily paper and the picture of Dad. Coppers either side of him. Bundling him along. Bundling him into the police van.

'You bastard,' I whispered. 'Bastard.' I didn't care about him being sent down for life. I didn't care. Because as far back as I can remember I've always hated him. All he ever seemed to do was lay into me and Sheen. That's when he wasn't laying into our mum. Or if he wasn't laying into us he was always so hard and cold. A real tough nut. Yer know, you always had to be on the watch-out for him. Just in case. Just in case. Just in case he might explode. Hell it was. So we always tried to avoid him. Be where he wasn't. But he knew we did that, so sometimes he'd just make us sit in the lounge with him or something. Just so that he could have a real good laugh. That's all it was for. And once, me and Sheen, we decided to run. Skip it. We were going to find Micky and stay with him. But that pig got together a few of his mates and they searched for us. Then we were brought home and he beat the hell out of us with his bloody belt. So we never tried skipping it again. We just had to stay.

Dad was always organizing jobs. And sometimes he'd be away for a month at a time. So that used to give me and Sheen a break. But although he beat Mum up as well, she'd always tell on us if we did anything to upset her while he was away. She used to enjoy scaring us like that. Stupid cow. But she was just as frightened of him as we were.

But it was right weird. If ever we got into fights outside, or trouble, and the Law came round, Dad would always stick up for us. And then he'd ask us what happened, and as long as we came out on top all the time he used to be real chuffed.

'That's what I've been trying to beat into yer,' he used to say. 'The strength to look after yourself. Because that's the only way you'll be successful and survive.'

He used to make me feel really proud sometimes, the way he spoke like that. And it was the only thing about him that I understood. But it was a lot of crap really. Everything was. The whole family. All a lot of crap. Except for Sheen and Micky, that was. If it hadn't been for them I would have done away with myself before now. Sure as hell I would.

'Hey, Teens. Come up and I'll show you our room.' Sheen poked her head round the door. 'Come on. It ain't bad.'

It wasn't a bad room. Pretty smart, yer know. Large too. With a couple of single beds. And it was decorated in a lemon colour and it had white-wooded wardrobes and a dressing-table in the same wood.

'We've even got our own record player,' Sheen

enthused. 'It ain't nothing special, but at least it's a record player.'

'Great.'

'Hey, what's wrong?'

I lugged one of my suitcases on the bed and opened it. I didn't answer her.

'Hey, Teens.' She wrapped an arm around me. 'Hey, Teens, come on. We're on to a shiner here.'

'You've made yourself at home.'

'We're on to a shiner, girl.'

'Yeah, sure.'

'That guy's a bleeding walkover. I tell yer. We've got it made. Hell, we've walked into this one, Teens. We really have. He says we can get settled in before we look for jobs. He'll give us a couple of months.'

'You gonna change, then?'

'What the hell you talking about?'

'Getting all chummy with them, weren't yer?'

'Man, you don't know that we've got it made. We can afford to get all chummy with them.'

I started unpacking my case. Taking out the clothes. Finding hangers in one of the wardrobes. Hanging them up.

All the while Sheena was buzzing around the room like an excited bumblebee. 'We got it made. We got it made,' she kept on singing. I didn't know why she was so happy.

'It's all gonna be so different.' I lay on the bed Sheen said was mine. 'And Micky's just bunged us in here. We haven't even had time to think about it.'

'Just don't worry, darling. Don't worry.'

'So, what's gonna happen to us, eh? What's gonna happen?'

'We'll just be the same.'

'What did Micky mean?'

'Emotional he was getting. Emotional.'

'He said we've got to take this chance.'

'Yeah, he's right. We can bleeding screw this lot. Get just what we want if we play it right. Yeah, we'll take this chance.'

'Micky never meant it like that.'

'Micky's gone, Teens. Why the hell should we suck up to him all the time? Have yer seen the silver stuff he's got downstairs? We can take that to Billy and get a load for it.'

'Yeah, and get done for it.'

'We won't get done. I told yer, he's soft. Soft.'

'Anyway, it's all talk. Ain't it?'

'Piss off. I'll show yer.'

'Sure.'

I sighed. Turned on to my stomach. How things could change. A few hours ago it was Sheena hating the thought of staying with our uncle and me not minding. But now the situation was completely reversed. I hated the idea and Sheena didn't mind. And yet I used to dream about being a member of a different family. A happy family. I used to write stories about it. About me being one of those girls who never did anything wrong and who never got into any fights. About having a father who really loved me. I used to dream about it. But now I felt scared. Just scared of being somewhere different. I felt scared of change. Too scared. I didn't want anything to change. I didn't want my dreams to come true.

'You just gotta make the best out of every situation, Tina. All the time, that's what you gotta do. Anyway, you coming downstairs? I'm gonna get something else to eat outta them.'

'No. I'm staying here.'
'See yer, then.'
'See yer.'

Chapter 4

When I woke the next morning I wondered where I was. But then I remembered and when I remembered I felt really heavy. As if I was sinking in the bed. Down and down. Down and down. I wished I was back home. In my old bedroom. I wished I could hear Dad in the bathroom. I wished I could feel that fear I always felt when I woke up on Sunday morning. That fear which made me always get quickly out of bed to go downstairs and make everyone breakfast. I did that always before Dad had the chance to drag me out. Before Dad had the chance. Before Dad had the chance.

'Wake up.' Sheen chucked a pillow at me. 'Wake up. Time for church,' she mocked.

'Get lost.'

'Ain't yer coming to church?'

'Stuff it, Sheena.'

'Our Father who art in heaven.'

She made me laugh then because she was kneeling on her bed with her hands held together. Like a bloody nun she looked, with a part of the sheet draped over her head.

'What's the time?'

'Half past nine.' She threw another pillow at me. 'Come on, get up. They all go to church in a minute. We'll have a chance to go through the place.'

'Hey, isn't it strange?'

'What?'

'Being somewhere different.'

'Hey.' Sheen suddenly jumped out of bed. And grabbed me. Pretending to be our dad. Shaking me. 'Hey, get out of bed. You lazy slut. Go and make breakfast. D'you want my belt round you? Go on. Get up.' Then Sheen started tickling me and we had a friendly fight. Bouncing on both beds and larking about. Like two dogs we were sometimes. And it was a good feeling. Wild, you know. Real wild.

'Don't let it get to yer, Teens.'

I was lying on the bed and Sheen was sitting on top of me. We were both knackered. She was stroking my hair.

'Don't let nothing get to yer in this place. It's no hassle, yer know. We can deal with it.'

I held her hand. 'Our dad murdered someone, Sheen.'

'What the hell.'

'I wonder what it feels like.'

'Forget him.'

'I wish he'd never done that, so we could be the same as before.'

'And you always said that all you wanted was a way out.'

'Yeah.'

'I'm glad we could get out of there.'

'But that means it's all over. Mum, Dad, us. It's all over.'

'It was over years ago, darling.'

'But, at least, although none of us liked it there we still had it. We knew about it. We knew how to cope with Dad.'

'Keep out of his way.'

'So? We knew how to cope.'

'Who wants to cope with that?'

'At least we knew.'

'Just don't worry, Teens. Don't worry. We'll be OK. We'll be fine.'

'Sure?'

'Yeah, 'course I'm sure. We'll be OK. Come on. Let's change.'

'It just feels different.'

'Come on. Let's change.' Sheen chucked my clothes at me. 'Let's change.'

When we got downstairs they'd all gone to church, so me and Sheen were alone. There was a note on the table saying that we could have whatever we wanted for breakfast. All we had to do was find it. So we found some eggs and bacon and had them.

'OK, let's have a hunt round,' Sheen said when we'd finished. 'They won't be back yet.'

'Where we gonna start?'

'Let's start upstairs.'

So me and Sheen, up we went and opened the first door we came to. It was on the left, past the stairs.

'It looks like Daniel's room.'

'Daniel?'

'The swot of the house. He's taking A-levels or something.'

It was a room smaller than our one. It had old-fashioned-type furniture in it and a mahogany desk.

'School books, see?' Sheen said.

Piles of them on the desk.

'What's in the drawers?' I loved opening drawers. You know, it's always a surprise to find what people keep in them. The drawers of his desk weren't very exciting, though. Just pens and pencils. Scraps of paper. A diary. More school books. I did see a good biro, though. A gold Papermate biro. I took it. Put it in my pocket.

'Hey, look at this radio, special, eh.' Sheen started fiddling with it. Then she just snapped the aerial off. Just like that. She opened a small box.

'What's he got in there?' I had a look too.

Cross and chain.

'Rubbish,' Sheen said.

'Wouldn't Billy like a gold cross and chain?'

'Fifty pence he'd give us.'

'Maybe we could get more for it, though. Sell it to one of the crowd? Yeah?'

'OK. Take it.'

So I slid that into my back pocket, along with the pen.

'Hi.' A voice came from nowhere.

'Bloody hell!' Didn't we both jump. If pigs could fly my hair was standing on end.

'Hi.' Just like that.

Sheen spun round. Just like a fiery rat. Her eyes alight. Ready to attack, she was. Make a run for it or something. Hell, I didn't know what to do. So, I just stood there looking at the girl in the doorway. She had faded blue jeans on, just like ours, and a white tee-shirt. She had long black hair.

'Hi,' she said again.

I looked at Sheen to see what move she'd make.

'Hi,' Sheen said. 'We were just making ourselves at home, yer know. Yer should have knocked before entering. It's rude to just barge in. Anyway, we're through now, ain't we, Teens?'

'Yeah, we're through.' I tried to sound as tough as my sister. And then I followed her past the girl and down the stairs. Into the kitchen. And I sat on the table because Sheen did so.

The girl followed us. 'Wanna cup of tea?' she asked. 'I'm making one.'

'Yeah, I'll have a cup.' Sheen still sounded tough. I knew it had got to her. The girl catching us like that. When we'd been so damn sure we had the whole house to ourselves. I knew Sheen was probably sulking because the girl had spoilt our plans. Well, we couldn't rout through the rest of the place with her there, could we?

I tell you, though. I felt my back pocket just to make sure the cross and the pen were still there, and when I found they were, I felt pleased with my catch. Real chuffed like.

'Which one's Sheena and which one's Tina?' the girl asked, after she'd filled the kettle with water and switched it on.

'I'm Sheena.'

'I wasn't sure if you were identical twins or not. The last time we saw each other I reckon we were all kids. I'm Rebecca, by the way. Dad's eldest. I don't live at home, normally. Only at the moment I am because my bedsit's being redecorated.'

'You ain't got a mum, have yer?'

'No.'

'Why?'

'Because she died, of course.'

'Because she died, of course,' Sheena mimicked.

Rebecca shrugged. Took three mugs out of the cupboard.

'Mum thought church was a load of crap and that vicars only liked being vicars 'cos they think they're God's gift.'

I smiled inside. Sheen was really laying it on thick Right narked she was about having Rebecca catching us. And that's why she was laying it on. I loved it, though, when Sheen got going. She knew just what to say. Just how to play it.

'Does your dad reckon himself?' she said.

Rebecca didn't answer. The kettle boiled.

'You don't say much, do yer?'

'I do when I've something to say.'

Sheen laughed. And then jumped off the table. 'Come on, Teens. Let's get out of here.'

'What about our tea?' But I jumped off the table.

'Sod the tea. Come on.'

So we buggered off out.

'Stupid cow,' Sheen mumbled.

'Where we going?'

We picked up our crash helmets so we could get on our bikes and go where the hell we liked.

'Wow-ee.' Sheen whistled and stood stock-still.

I followed her gaze and saw what she was looking at. 'Bloody hell!'

'Who's is that?'

It was a Kawasaki. Gleaming red and black. A Kawasaki 1000.

'Whose is it?' Sheen repeated. Walking over to it. 'What a beauty.'

'Micky would love that.' I walked round the bike. Like a gentle, loving monster it looked. Putting our bikes to shame.

'Hey, Teens.'

'What?'

'Yer don't reckon, do yer?'

'What?'

'That it's hers.'

Hers? Hers! 'Rebecca's?'

'Well, who else's could it be? Parked here. In front of their house.'

'Maybe it's hers.'

'Come on. Let's go and see.' Sheen was all excited then. Motorbikes always made her excited. But when I thought of how Sheen had acted to Rebecca just a few minutes earlier – Hell, a motorbike could make all the difference. Motorbikes, fighting and crime were the only things that made Sheena completely excited. And when it came to those everything else went to pot. Everything else was forgotten.

I followed Sheen, at a charge, back into the kitchen.

'Hey, is that your bike out there?' she asked.

Rebecca was sitting, drinking tea. She looked pleased to see us back again. 'Yeah, that's my bike.'

'Your Kawasaki 1000?'

'Yeah. All mine.'

'Bleeding hell, that's some machine.'

'I totally agree with you.' She smiled. Holding out her hand then, and Sheen shook it. I did the same.

'You ride with anyone?' Sheen asked.

'Yeah. Sometimes.'

'Any chapters?'

'No. Nothing like that.'

'Our brother, Micky, used to ride with a chapter.'

'What bike did he have?'

'Oh, Micky used to go through bikes like shampoo. He was always writing them off. Old English bikes mostly. The last bike he had, though, was a 750 Suzy. But he ain't got one no more.'

'How long have you had yours?' Rebecca looked

at me, but I waited for Sheen to answer.

'Six months. Micky bought them for us. Just like that. Didn't he, Teens?'

'Yeah.' I remembered. It was money from a job but that didn't matter. 'And he taught us to ride them proper. We've both passed our test.'

'Hey, what about that then, a bleeding vicar's daughter an' all. I bet your old man nearly shit himself when you brought that home.'

'He went a bit mad, but I'd left home by then so he couldn't do much about it. He doesn't mind too much now though. I've given him a spin on it a couple of times. He likes it really. He just won't admit it.'

'Bloody hell, a vicar on a Kawasaki 1000.' Sheena snorted.

'Don't just think of him as a vicar,' Rebecca said. 'He's a man before he's a vicar. Just an ordinary man.'

'Hey, how about you coming out for a burn up with us?' Sheen suggested. 'That's where me and Teen were going. You coming too?'

'Well, I would like to, but we tend to treat Sundays as a family day. In between church we usually stay in. That's when we get the chance to be all together. And anyway I'm cooking the Sunday dinner today. We'd really love it for you to stay in as well. Dinner's at one, but apart from that we'd like you to be with us.'

'Aaah, we go and see our mates on Sundays.'

'Yeah,' I chipped in. 'We go to a coffee place in Sugbridge. All our mates are there. We get food too, yer know. Free food, 'cos the owner knows our brother.'

'OK. Sure. That's fine. Just as long as you know you're welcome, that's all.'

'Anyway, another time we'll go for a burn up,' Sheen enthused.

'Yeah. Another time.'
'OK, let's split, Teens. See yer, Rebecca.'
'See yer.'

Chapter 5

Jon's café wasn't actually in Sugbridge town but on the outskirts. At the end of a small row of shops it was. Next to a bookmaker's. It was our place, yer know? Jon's café. We were sort of the top dogs there. Well, apart from Micky was there. Jon owned the place. He was a good mate of Micky's. He never got into much trouble with the Law, though, but he was all right, Jonny. He'd never grass on no one anyway. And he was fat and cuddly. We often made fun of his fat paunch.

'Hiya, kids.' Sheen walked into the café. It was full of round tables and wooden chairs. There was a juke box and two video games down one side of it.

The café was pretty full as usual. With mostly kids. We knew all of them, Sheen and I. They looked up to us. I s'pose it was partly because we had a dad like we had and partly because of Micky. They respected Micky for always doing things wrong and never getting caught. They thought that was great. But me and Sheen, we'd proved ourselves to be as tough as Micky. In fights and that. We'd earned the kids' respect on our own. Individually. Without Micky or Dad's influence. And they were scared of us really, the kids. They knew we both carried knives and weren't afraid to use them.

'Anyone want to buy a gold cross and chain?' I approached a couple of tables with about six guys and four girls sitting around. Most of those were older than me and Sheen, but they respected us just the same. Age made no difference. That's why I went to them, because they were older and likely had more cash than the younger kids.

'How much?' Tim asked.

'Five quid to you.'

Tim took the cross and chain. Studying it. Then he passed it to David and it slowly went round everyone.

'I've got to buy a birthday present for me sister,' Sharon said. 'It would be OK for her, wouldn't it, Terry?'

Her boyfriend nodded his head.

'I'll have it then.' She made up her mind. 'Five quid?'

'Yeah. A fiver and it's yours.'

So that was how I made a fiver that morning. Simple. Just like that. A fiver in me pocket.

'Wotcher, Jonny.'

'Hello, Tina. All right?'

'OK.' I sat on a stool by the counter.

'How you settling in?'

'Micky told yer, did he?'

'Yeah. He was in here after he dropped you off yesterday.'

'D'you know where he went?'

'Not a sign, love. Micky wouldn't let on. Not to anyone.'

'See what our dad got?'

'Heard it on the news last night.'

'I bet there was only one topic of conversation in here last night.'

'You could be right,' Jon smiled. 'Anyway, how are you settling in?'

I shrugged. 'All right, I s'pose. Did Micky seem in a weird mood to you yesterday?'

'In a reflective mood. I s'pose he was. Cut up about yer dad, though.'

'I was surprised Micky went to see the court case. He's always hated him.'

'Your old man broke down in court, Tina. Did Micky tell you that?'

'What?'

'He broke down. Said he never meant to kill no one. Said it was all a mistake. Said he only took the shooter along to threaten.'

'Hey, you're talking out of the back of your head.'

'Truth. Your old man broke. He was in tears.'

'That's a lot of crap.' My old man would never break down. Would never cry. No. Not for anyone.

'No, it's not a lot of crap.' Micky saw him cry. That's what was eating at Micky.'

'My old man would never cry. You don't know him.'

'Didn't you read the papers?'

'No. Just saw the picture.'

'Well, if you read . . .'

'You mean it was all in the papers?'

'And on the news.'

Anger swirled inside me. Like a giant volcano. Erupting. Slowly. Slowly. Erupting. 'Bloody pig. What the hell did he wanna go and do that for? Everyone will know now.' I could just imagine it. 'Your old man cried. Your old man cried and when we all thought he was so tough and so hard.'

'Bloody hell!' I banged my hand on the counter. Making a spoon jump out of a saucer. 'What a bastard.'

'Perhaps he really did never mean to murder anyone.'

'Of course he meant to. He loves hurting people, don't he? He loves laying into them. So murdering's no different, is it? Murdering's no different.'

'Well, you wouldn't know that, would you, love?'

I swung away from the counter. Absolutely livid. I wondered what the hell all the kids in the café thought about it. I bet to hell they were laughing behind our backs. I bet to hell they were. Well, I'd show them. I'd show them who's the hardest. Who's the toughest. I'd show them.

I shoved one of the kids out of his chair. 'OK,' I yelled, picking up the chair, 'OK, who the hell was it then? One of you did it.'

lence echoed in the café. Faces turned to me. All shocked. All surprised.

l, I ain't taking any of that from none of yer.' ice hurled away from me. As if it was a rocket the launch pad.

'OK, I wanna know who laughed at my old man. I know it was one of you so you'd better just stand up right now and take what's coming to yer.'

'Tina, I don't have no trouble in here,' Jonny said.

'Shut it, Jonny. It ain't got nothing to do with you.'

'Yeah, shut yer mouth, Jonny,' Sheena snarled. Coming across to me then. 'What's up then, Teens? What these kids been doing?'

'Laughing at our old man,' I yelled. And slammed the chair onto the floor again and again until two of the legs broke off. I picked up one of the legs and smashed it onto a table, where the kids all jumped away. I grabbed one of them. Stevie was his name. I grabbed him and shoved him over to Sheena. He fell on the floor. 'It could have been him, Sheen.'

'No, it never. It never was me.' He was kneeling on the floor. Pleading like a whipped dog. 'It never was me. I never laughed at your old man. Honest. Honest. I . . .'

Sheena kicked him. Right in the stomach she kicked him. So I did too. Up his backside. Twice I did it.

'OK. So who's next?' Sheen shouted. Walking around the tables. Then she grabbed another boy. She grabbed him by the hair. While she was doing that some other kids made a run for it. About eight of them went.

'Harry. Clive. Get after them.' I gave my orders to a group sitting by the window. They weren't kids. They were leaders too. Coming just after me and Sheen. When we weren't around they gave the orders. But they took orders as well. From us. They all went out of the door. Six of them. Quicker than Sheen had belted that other kid round the face.

Then I noticed two of the other older boys had moved a table in front of the door and sat on it to stop any more of the kids from escaping.

'OK,' I yelled. 'We take one of you at a time. That's what we're gonna do. 'Cos if the person don't own up, you're all gonna suffer for it.' I slammed that wooden leg against another table. Crockery smashed. Drinks spilt.

'We're gonna do the lot of yer,' Sheen screamed. ''Cos you're all a load of tripe. You ain't worth nothing. Nothing. None of you are.'

'I did it. I laughed. It was me.'

He was a long, skinny boy. Ginger hair and ginger freckles. Fifteen he was. His name was Tommy White. 'It was me. I laughed at yer dad. I did. I'm sorry, OK?'

Sheen jumped over a chair and grabbed him. Christ, she really kneed him between the legs. He went down like a deflated balloon. Then she dragged him across the floor.

'OK, you bastard.' I got in on the act. Feeding on the fear. Feeding on the silence. On our power. 'You're gonna see what you get if you ever laugh at any of our family. Or crack jokes about them. I'm gonna show you what you're gonna get.'

I took the stick I was holding in my hand and brought it down across the back of his legs. Again and again I did it. Hearing the crunch of wood against skin. Wood against bone. The kid was screaming. Every time I hit him he yelled but it made me carry on. I liked making him scream. It was good.

Then Sheen carried a bucket of water out of the kitchen. And we yanked the kid up and held his head under the water for a few seconds.

'You ain't never gonna laugh at our old man again,' Sheena growled at the boy. Between each of the dippings. 'You ain't never gonna laugh at our old man again. You ain't never gonna laugh at our old man again. You ain't never gonna laugh at our old man again.' Dip. Dip. Dip. Dip. Dip. Dip.

Splutter. Splutter. Cough. Cough.

'That's it,' I said. 'Bloody choke up.'

Then Sheen laid into him with her boot. Right in the face she got him. And blood spurted all over the floor.

'OK?' She turned to me.

'A beauty.'

'Let's split then.'

The other older boys followed us out. It felt great, yer know. As if we were something real special. The way the boys flanked us on our way over to our motorbikes. They never said nothing. None of us did. We just revved our bikes and were away. All ten of us. And they were all following Sheen and me. Without saying anything, they were just following.

It was great, though. Riding along in a group. Kings of the road, we were. Pedestrians stopped to gawp at us. So we did V signs to them. Nosy pigs they were.

I was surprised when Sheen pulled into a lay-by, but I followed her in. The rest of our mob did too. And then I was even more surprised when Sheen told everyone else to go their own way.

They all went. Leaving just me and Sheen.

'What the hell did you do that for?' I got off Lobby. Followed Sheen to a grass park which was next to our stopping place. 'What the hell did you tell them to split for? We've got the rest of the day.'

'What the hell am I doing?' She yanked off her crash helmet and threw it on the ground. 'What am I doing? What the hell were you doing?' She faced me. Her eyes livid.

'Me?'

'Yes, you.' She shoved me. Made me drop my helmet.

'Hey, watch it.'

'Me. Watch it! What were you bloody doing? Back at Jonny's. You stupid bitch.'

'You know what I was doing.'

''Cos they laughed at our old man?'

'Yeah. That's right. The kid said so, didn't he?'

'You're crazy. Who told yer he laughed? Jonny never. You never knew before yer went in there. None of the kids would have grassed.'

'OK.' I turned away from her. Just wanting to breathe. Fresh air. Fill my lungs.

'OK, so?' She grabbed my arm. 'So? No one told yer, did they?'

'But he laughed, didn't he? He said.'

'I tell yer something, kid. Our father might cry in court, but he ain't bloody crazy.'

'What d'yer mean, he ain't crazy? Nor am I crazy and how the hell d'you know about him crying?'

'You might just look at the pretty photos but I read the print as well.'

'So, you knew?'

'Of course.'

'So you wanted to do that kid as much as I wanted to do him.'

'You know, when people are crazy they think people are laughing at them. They don't know. They ain't got no proof. But that's how madness takes them. They think people are laughing at them.'

I shoved her. Real hard. I shoved her.

'Listen. Micky would have never accused without being a hundred per cent certain. He never made up reasons for attacking.'

'You did it too.'

'I had to come in with yer. Once you'd started. But we were lucky someone did laugh at Dad. 'Cos if no one had've done you would have been a right bum.'

'They wouldn't have known. They would have accused each other.'

'But you would have known. And knowing you made a mistake would have made you weaker. Don't make no mistakes. That's what Micky used to say. Don't put your own strength in jeopardy. Be right all the time. Right in yer own mind. Then yer can be strong enough to beat all of them.'

'But I was right. He laughed.'

'You never knew that, though. Not before you went in. Anyway, what the hell, he laughed. I wouldn't have done him over for that. Let him laugh when we're not around. But if he laughs when we're around and when we hear what he's laughing at, then we can lay into him. What's a laugh when we're not around? It doesn't hurt us. Your trouble is you ain't got enough confidence in yerself. You don't think you can be as tough as you need to be.'

'Of course I think I can be as tough as I need to be. I know I can be that tough. I am tough. I know, OK?'

'No trouble in Jonny's place. That's what Micky says. No trouble in Jonny's place. We don't want the Law in there, do we? You stupid cow.'

'You're a right one to talk about what Micky says. You said that we don't have to hang on Mick's word no more.'

'That's when he talks a lot of emotional crap.'

'When he talks about us going straight?'

She hit me then. Punched me. I went down but only for a minute. I hit her back. She hit me again and we were in a scrap then. I fought like hell but she's a wild bloody cat. And I really wanted to beat her then. More than anything. I tried with all my strength, all my life, to beat her. But she was too strong.

I was on the ground. And she was kicking all hell out of me. At my spine. My legs. My stomach. My arms where I was shielding my face and head. Then she had hold of my hair and was yanking back my head.

'Micky said nothing about us going straight. You get that into your thick bleeding head. He said nothing about us going straight.'

She left me then. My body was hurting all over. My

face was bleeding. I tried to lift my head from the muddy grass but everything started to spin. Round and round. Round and round. Like cars on a race-track.

I heard Sheen's bike start and then I heard it disappear. Tears were coming from my eyes but I wasn't crying. It was just pain. And the fact that Sheena had done me over. Hell, I felt so angry. Deep inside I was so angry. Because I hadn't beaten her. I could never beat her. She was always the strongest and I was always scared of her. Because she was a crazy bitch, that's why I was scared of her. She knew no limits, see. She just kicked until she ran out of steam. Or got fed up. She never gave a damn about the other person. She wouldn't even care if they were dying. God, I tried to be like her. I really tried. Every minute of every day. So that it could be me the one without fear and not her.

I sat and gradually the dizziness left me. I found my cigarettes and lit one. I spat out blood from my mouth and wiped it away from my face. But it still trickled down. It was just under my right eye where the blood was coming from.

I felt so humiliated, yer know. All I wanted to do was disappear. Just go. Anywhere. Somewhere. Just to not be Tina Rudy any more. Just to blow that girl out of all existence.

Yer know, I felt like I felt after Dad used to hit me with his belt. Yer know, Sheen would never be like me after a beating. She'd just struggle up and go downstairs again. Just to try and prove to him that he hadn't hurt her. Yer knew it would make her get even tougher. But me, I just used to lie there, feeling just as I did then. Humiliated. Sick. Sick. Gut sick. And I just used to wish I was someone else completely different.

I never could fight the pain like Sheen did, just to prove her point. I always used to be too beaten for that.

It was quarter past one by the time I managed to get back on my bike again. I started my machine and knew there was only one place I could go where I would be away from the chance of bumping into my mates who would immediately know I'd been done over. Only one place I could go. Back to Lower Radford. Back to my bedroom.

Chapter 6

I went in through the back door leading to the kitchen. It was empty, but you could see someone had been cooking a Sunday dinner. I heard voices from the dining room as I crept up the stairs. But no one disturbed me.

The bed was soft and comforting to my body. I lay there, smoking another fag and listening to the silence.

I'm sick of being beaten, I thought. And then I thought of the ginger-haired guy we'd done over. I'd hit him hard. Real hard. Hating him all the time I was hitting. Hating him for laughing. And yet Sheena hadn't given a fig about him laughing. She really hadn't. Yer know, sometimes I just couldn't understand Sheena. All I understood was that she couldn't be beaten. And if she had to she'd fight until her own death. That's all I understood about Sheena.

I jumped when there was a knock at the door. And then Uncle Howard came in.

'Hello,' he smiled. 'I thought I heard someone creep up the stairs.'

'Hi,' I watched him as he moved a chair and sat by the side of my bed. I felt nervy, yer know, with him there like that. I wondered what the hell he was playing at. But then I didn't really care what he was playing at. He could do what the hell he liked. It was his house.

'What's happened to you, then?'
I didn't answer.
'You look pretty bruised.'
'I'm OK.'
'You are?'
'Yeah, I'm OK.'
'I get worried when my kids come home with physical injuries. Rebecca calls me a nagging mother.'
'I ain't yer kid.'
'I'd like to think of you as a member of my family now.'
'Think what yer like.'
'Come on, tell me what happened, Tina.'
I said nothing.
'No?'
'I'm OK.'
'Who did you fight with?'
'Sheena.' I shouldn't have told him, I s'pose. Yer know, some things have to be kept strictly within the family. But I couldn't be bothered just then. I couldn't be bothered to hold anything back. Everything could go to hell. And Sheena could too. I felt really sick of Sheena then. And sick of her codes of living. I thought they were all a load of tripe.
'You had a fight with Sheena?' He sounded surprised.
'Yeah.'
'I thought you two were like that.' He crossed his fingers.
'Only when it suits Sheena we're like that.'
'What was it about?'
'I just did something she didn't like.' That was all. Basically.
'Is there a moral to that?'

'What?'

'Never do what Sheena doesn't want you to do. Or is it always do what Sheena wants you to do?'

I didn't answer.

'Come on. Come downstairs. To the kitchen. I'll put something on that eye of yours.'

'No. Honest. It's OK. I don't need nothing on it.'

'Come on. It won't do you any harm, will it? Eh?' He smiled at me then. Touched me head. 'Come on. If my parishioners see you with an eye like that they'll think I've been beating you up.'

I followed him downstairs. Yer know, it was kind of nice having someone who wants to do something for you. Something sort of kind.

'Sit down.' He pulled a stool out for me. 'Now let's see. Ice. That's what we need.'

I watched him find a clean tea-towel in the drawer, then he went to the fridge and pulled out a tray of ice cubes.

Then a young girl came in carrying a load of dinner plates.

'Oh, is it all right to start clearing up now, Dad?'

'Can you wait until we've finished, honey? There's plenty of time.'

'What're you doing?'

'Making an ice pack. This is Tina. Have you two met each other? Tina, Jilly, my youngest. Ten.'

'Hello,' I said to her.

'Hi.' Then she stared at my eye for a while and looked confused but didn't say anything about it. 'Dad, can I go out and play football?'

'You've just had your dinner. Let it settle. You can help with the drying up first.'

'But you said we've got to wait.'

'Wait a while.'

'How long?'

'Don't be impatient.'

'Can I have some more pudding then while I'm waiting?'

'If you want.'

'Shall I dish some more out for you?'

'No, darling, I don't want any more, I've had enough.'

'OK. But don't be long.'

Uncle Howard took out the ice cubes and put them in the tea-towel. I thought we were going to be alone again then, but the boy came in.

'What yer doing, Dad?' he said, bouncing around the table. 'Hi, nice to meet you again.' He held out his hand to me. 'I'm Daniel. Second in line to the throne. Seventeen years old. A farm labourer. Sorry, a part-time farm labourer. When I'm not at school,' he recited.

'Daniel.' Uncle Howard looked agitated.

'Wow, you've got a shiner,' Daniel said, peering at my eye, as if he was a doctor or something.

'Yeah and if you move yourself I can put this on it,' Uncle Howard said.

'How d'yer get it?'

'Fighting.'

'Aaaah, boy, you've got Dad in his element now, Tina. It is Tina, isn't it?'

'Yeah.'

'I thought so. Sheena's the hard case. You've got Dad in his element. He's a frustrated doctor, that's what he is. Come home with a cut and he'll lay you in bed for a fortnight.'

'Don't take any notice of him, Tina. He's only being

sarcastic because when he comes home with a little cut he wants a lot of attention and I don't give it to him.'

'As you'll soon see, Tina,' Daniel said, 'I'm the left-out one of this family. Even if I had a broken leg he wouldn't care, you know. Just walk right past, he would.'

'That's right.' Uncle Howard smiled at me, winking. 'Now, Tina. This might sting a bit at first.' Uncle Howard put the ice pack against my eye and held it there. I felt a bit awkward with him holding it there like that. Tense, yer know.

'Here, you hold it,' he said. 'Make sure you keep it on there. It doesn't matter if the water dribbles.'

'And he's always moaning at us about getting his kitchen floor dirty,' Daniel said, going out of the kitchen. 'Life just isn't fair.'

'That's Daniel,' Uncle Howard said. 'You won't be able to miss Daniel.'

I sat there with the ice pack on my eye while the others cleared away the dinner stuff around me. Rebecca came out and helped too, and she said there was a dinner left for me if I wanted it. I said I did. But Uncle Howard told me to wait a bit longer with the ice pack on my eye before I ate it. So I went into the lounge and sat on the settee. Jilly was the only one not helping with the washing of the dishes. She was stretched out on the floor reading a comic. She turned round when I went in, though, and looked at me.

'Were you in a fight?' she asked.

'Yeah.'

'Did you win?'

I shrugged.

'I got in a fight last week at school. But don't tell

Dad. He hates me fighting. I did win, though. The other girl started to cry.'

I smiled then. She made me smile. 'Why did yer fight?' I asked.

'Oh, this girl was really getting on my nerves. She's teacher's pet, see? I hate teachers' pets.'

'Yeah.'

'D'you hate teachers' pets?'

'Yeah.'

'They're real creeps.'

'Aren't you a creep then?'

'No way. I hate school. It's so boring.'

'I hate creeps too.'

'Did you used to fight at school?'

'Yeah.'

'Did you swear?'

'At school?'

'Yeah.'

'Yeah.'

'At home?'

'No.'

'The other day I got sent to the headteacher for swearing at school and then when I came home Dad sent me up to my room for swearing at the dinner table. Phew, all in one day. All that trouble. Too much.'

'What d'yer say?'

'How did I swear?'

'Yeah.'

She quickly shut the lounge door. And then knelt in front of me, whispering, 'I said piss off at school and shit at home.'

I laughed at that.

'Dad can't stand me swearing. He blasphemes,

though. Daniel says blaspheming is worse than swearing. Rebecca hates me swearing as well, although she used to swear. When she went away for two years she swore.'

'Rebecca's got a motorbike, hasn't she?'

'Yeah. Have you seen it?'

'Um.'

'I'm getting one as soon as I can. I've been on the back of hers.'

'Yeah?'

'A couple of times. When Dad's not around. But then he caught us once. And he was annoyed with us for two whole weeks after that. And it's good, 'cos when Dad gets annoyed with Rebecca she gets annoyed with him. And they really get mad with each other. They're as stubborn as each other, that's what Daniel says. But Rebecca, she's great, have you heard about her?'

'What d'yer mean, heard about her?'

'She's been in the paper. And she's going to be on the telly.'

'Why?'

'She runs this centre for the unemployed. Well, people help her, but she's the main one. She started it all. And lots of kids who get into trouble with the police go there.'

That made me start. Guilty conscience and all that.

'Anyway, how she got in the paper was something happened to this girl. It's a long story. I don't know it all. But Rebecca got to saying all about the centre and everything. How she's trying to help the people who get in trouble with the police. And what she's doing. And then loads of important people started ringing her up. And she's nearly famous now.'

'Wow.' I was taking the piss out of Jilly then. Because she sounded so excited about Rebecca. About her nearly being famous. 'But I ain't never heard of her. So she can't be that famous.'

'Well, she's nearly famous, anyway. But she doesn't really want to be famous. She just wants to help, that's all.'

'Great.'

'She's only been back for ten months, though.'

'Back?' It was getting pretty interesting. All this about Rebecca. What she was doing and all that. It was pretty interesting.

'Yeah. She went away travelling for two years. When she was nineteen. She had a row with Dad and just walked out. For two years she never even wrote home or nothing. Dad was worried about her but he said he couldn't go after her because that wasn't what she wanted.'

'Where'd she go?'

'All places. Abroad mostly. She was sort of different when she came back, though. Then she moved out. She's friends with Dad now, though. As long as they don't see too much of each other they're all right.'

I said nothing. Just moved the ice pack on my eye to a different position. It was sort of weird hearing about their family. It was as if it brought me closer to them in a way. Closer, in one way. I liked that feeling. It was warm.

'Do you like your dad?' she asked me.

'No.'

'Was your dad cruel?'

'Just a bit.'

'He's in prison now, isn't he?'

'Yeah.'

'Did he kill someone?'

'Yeah.'

'Wow. I wonder why.'

'Too hard to explain.'

'Was he a bastard?'

'He is a bastard. That's why he did it.'

'You said it was too hard to explain.'

'I thought you weren't allowed to swear.'

She frowned then. 'Did I swear?'

'Yeah. You said bastard.' And she knew she'd sworn. I could tell she knew.

She shrugged. 'I'm always doing things I shouldn't. Don't worry about it.'

'I ain't worried.'

Then the door opened and Daniel came in.

'Jilly, go and help with the wiping up. Your dinner's on the kitchen table, Tina. All burnt and shrivelled.' Then he bounced out again.

My dinner wasn't all burnt and shrivelled.

I ate it and then went upstairs to our bedroom.

I lay on my bed and played a while with my flick knife. Just fiddling about with it. Then I started thinking. About Uncle Howard. And thinking about him made me angry. Huh, I thought. Uncle Howard, pussy eyes. That's all he was really. Uncle Howard, pussy eyes. Nothing else to him. Pussy eyes. Pussy eyes. I hate pussy eyes. They make me spuke. Tra la, diddle dum. I held my flick knife in the air. Tra la, diddle dum. Diddle dum.

Then I felt like writing. So reached for my notepad and biro. I always kept them by my bed. Because I sometimes wrote things. Stupid things. Whatever came into my head. Anyway, what I did then was, on a fresh piece of paper I wrote:

UNCLE HOWARD, PUSSY EYES. NO GOOD PUSSY EYES.

Then I tore out the piece of paper, crept along the landing to his bedroom, went in and left the paper on his bed. Then I went back to my room again.

There was once a man called Howard, I wrote in my pad, who had a daughter. He was a bastard and she was a bitch. He had pussy eyes and she told loads of lies. Then I shut my pad, and shoved it under the bed. I never let anyone see the contents of my notepad. Even Sheena never saw inside.

I picked up a magazine which Rebecca had given to me to read and I sat and read it.

About an hour later Sheena returned. I was still reading that magazine. I didn't look at Sheena when she came in. Just carried on reading. A love story, it was, that I was in the middle of. A love story.

'Hey, Teens, I'm sorry I laid into yer so hard,' she said.

I didn't look up.

'Honest, Teens. I never meant to hit yer that hard.' She put her arm round me and kissed me head.

'It's OK.'

'You sulking with me?'

'No.'

'Friends then?'

I looked at her. Into her eyes.

'Friends, then?' she repeated.

'Yeah, friends.' We shook hands. And I was glad that we were friends again. I could never be sulky with Sheen for long. It just wasn't on.

'What you been doing?' she asked.

'Not much.'

'Where d'yer nick that from?'

'Rebecca gave it to me.'

'You been downstairs with them, then?'

'Yeah.'

'That's it. Get in there. Psych them out.'

'What's happening over Billy's?'

'That kid had to have stitches. The one I booted. Twelve stitches. And concussion.'

'Are the cops on to it?'

'No. Jonny took him up to the hospital. Told them he came off his push-bike.'

I didn't want to talk about that kid much. About him laughing and all that. I just wanted to forget.

'I was thinking,' Sheen said. Taking off her leather jacket. 'I was thinking. Maybe we'd better psych this town out an' all. Jim was telling me the pub to go to is The Hatchet. It ain't far from here. It's where all the big guys hang out.'

'Yeah?'

'Yeah. We'll go there tonight.'

'OK.'

Chapter 7

The pub was actually in the village of Lower Radford. On a corner, by the village green.

We parked our bikes outside on the road and walked into the public bar. It was only half past seven so it wasn't all that crowded.

'Two pints of lager,' Sheen ordered.

We sat on a couple of bar stools. I felt real comfortable then. The atmosphere in the pub was sort of bubbly. As if something could happen. Sheen stared around the bar, her eyes tense and suspicious. I looked too. There were three boys around the snooker table. They were in smart clothes. One of them had ginger hair and ginger freckles. There were a group of girls sitting on a table by the door. They were right tarts. Thick make-up. Short skirts. I could smell the stench of their perfume from where I was sitting. I really hated girls like that. They were giving me and Sheen sidelong glances, yer know. I caught one of the girls looking straight at me, so I stared her out.

There was a fat guy standing just along the bar from Sheen and me. He had dark, greasy hair. He was a hard case. He looked it, anyway. Reckon he didn't like no strangers going into the pub. Reckon there was a slight tension because me and Sheen were in there. That's what made it so exciting.

We just sat, though. Playing the hard, cool bit. Not giving a toss about any of them.

By half past nine the pub had filled up more. People had come in in dribs and drabs. People. Fellas. Girls. Hard cases. You could always tell the hard cases. They had a sort of air about them. Like me and Sheen. But it wasn't until quarter to ten that this guy came in. And the other hard cases were nothing compared to him. I'd guess he was in his thirties. He had blond hair. And a scar running down one side of his face. Really evil-looking he was. Like Dad. Exactly like Dad. His eyes were the same. As if they were made of metal instead of human matter. If he looked at you they could cut you in two. His eyes. The only difference between him and Dad was that this guy was wearing jeans and a tee-shirt. Dad used to always dress smart. In suits. He'd never wear jeans.

I felt Sheen tense beside me. She took another swig of her lager. The man walked to the bar. He stood right next to where I was sitting. The barman poured a whisky and just handed it to the man. He took that whisky down and asked for another.

Sheen lit two fags and handed me one. I could see she was getting wound up inside. I could tell because her eyes were beginning to go bloodshot. That always happened when Sheen got wound up. I knew why she was getting wound up. 'Cos the man walking in threatened her. The silence which followed him in. And because he was like Dad. I knew she was on the verge of doing something. And I was just waiting. And wondering what it was that she'd do. But I reckoned she'd have a job against this guy. A real job to out-cop him. But I knew Sheena didn't think that. 'Cos she was so wound up. And when she was like that she always thought she could win. Usually. She won. Usually.

When I felt a tap on my shoulder, I froze. Sheen looked at me. We were both facing towards the bar. I saw Sheen's hand go inside her jacket pocket. That was for her knife.

'Hi.'

What the hell! I turned round to that voice which I recognized. 'Hi.' I'd heard that voice somewhere before.

'Hi. Fancy seeing you here.' There was Rebecca. Rebecca, the vicar's daughter, smiling at me.

I just looked at her, yer know. So astounded that she was in there. I looked to see if she'd come in with anyone. But she was on her own.

'Well, I'll buy you a drink later.' She winked and then was gone. But not far. Only to the other side of that man, and she just was talking to him all friendly like and he was talking to her. No sweat.

'Hi, Dave,' she said, touching his shoulder.

'Hello, darling.' He smiled at her too. That man. With a scar. He actually smiled at Rebecca Holdaway.

'How are you?' she continued.

'Aaah, OK. You could say.'

'Liking it back with Jenny?'

'It's only been a week, ain't it?'

'Yeah. It's only been a week.'

'I might stick with her. I might not. What you having, Rebecca?'

'Martini and lemonade, please.'

The man ordered a drink for Rebecca. Bloody hell. Then the man, yer know, after Rebecca had got her drink, said,

'These two friends of yours?' Nodding his head to us.

And before I knew it Sheen snarled, 'No. We ain't

friends of hers. We ain't friends of no one round here.'

'You'd better clear off out then,' the man said. Not turning round.

'We'll clear off when we wanna clear off.'

Christ, I wondered what the hell Sheen was going to do. And I felt scared for her then. Tussling with that man. Real scared for her.

Rebecca butted in, though. 'They're my cousins, Dave. They're living with us,' and then, quieter, she said, 'They're OK.'

Sheen just smashed her glass on the bar. She did it again and again until glass was flying everywhere. Then she stood up. 'Come on then, big shot. Have a go at me.'

'Not tonight, darling. Not in front of Rebecca. She don't like fights.'

'Outside then.'

'Not tonight, I said.'

'Right. I'll see you around then, big guy. See you around.'

I followed Sheen outside into the fresh air. Into the darkness.

'Hell, Sheen. You real risked it that time.'

'Go for the big shot. All the time. Don't waste yourself on the second and third in line. Go for the top notch. Get in. Hit the top.'

'Reckon you'd beat him.'

'I'd give him another scar. Then it doesn't matter if I win or lose. That's all I wanna do. Give him another scar.'

'Yer know, sometimes I think you're crazy, Sheen. Real crazy.' And that was the truth. She was real crazy. Sometimes. Real crazy.

'What we doing now, Sheen?' I asked when we

were putting on our helmets. She was still het up and all. I could tell she was still het up.

'Let's go break a few windows.'

'Now?'

'Yeah, now.'

So that's what we did. We drove through the streets of Lower Radford first. Picking our houses. We only went for big houses. Yer know, where all the rich people lived. They were the best houses to do. Rich people. Huh. We could do them good and proper.

We picked a couple of houses and then we doubled back to a motorway construction site. There we found a couple of large bricks and shoved them down inside our jackets. Then we made our way back to the houses. They were down a cul-de-sac and it was real quiet down there. And dark.

There weren't any street lights. That's how me and Sheen liked it, though. When it was dark. There was less chance of being spotted.

We left our bikes on the main road just a few yards away from the cul-de-sac and then we walked. It was a great feeling. Real exciting. Walking along. Knowing you were going to smash a house.

'OK, you take this one and I'll take that,' Sheen said. So I stopped outside my house. It was large. Had blue shutters. I wondered who lived there. I watched Sheen as she stopped in front of her house. I knew the procedure. She'd count three to me on her fingers and then we'd run into the front gardens, chuck the bricks and then scarper. My stomach was really twirling while waiting for the count. The cold night air hit my cheeks.

I watched Sheen. First one finger. Then two. Three. That was it. The brick was in my hand. I jumped over their garden wall and hurled it towards a gleaming window. I heard the scream of effort coming from my mouth, the window smashing and then the alarm. I heard the same noises coming out of the blackness to the right of me. I was running then. My feet pounding on the pavement. My heart pounding within. Running. Running. I just prayed that Sheen was behind me.

She was.

We both leapt on our bikes.

'Come on, start, you bitch.' I kick-started my machine three times before she burst into life. But Sheen was off before me. Ever ready. Ever on top was Sheen. I followed her. Along the road. Past the street lights. I followed her as I felt the sweat trickle down the side of my face. As my heart gradually began to beat at more of a slow pace. I followed her.

We hit the roads and burnt off the cars. We travelled all the way to Stortford and then came back. Back to the vicarage.

Sheen was OK then. She'd got all that tension out of her.

It was quarter past eleven when we arrived back in the house. Uncle Howard had given Sheen a key, so we let ourselves in. It was all quiet.

'They must be in bed,' Sheen said.

'No.' I noticed a light shining underneath the lounge door.

'Let's go in then.' Sheen opened the lounge door and I went in after her.

Uncle Howard was sitting in there in pyjamas and a dressing gown. He was reading a book.

'Hello, girls,' he smiled.

'Hi,' Sheen said.

'Had a good night?'

'Yeah.' Sheen sat on the couch.

'Yeah, we've had a good night.' But, yer know, I didn't particularly feel like sitting down. Not with Uncle Howard. Not like that. I felt sick then, yer know. And had a knot in my stomach.

'I thought I'd wait up until I knew you were home again.'

'You needn't have bothered,' Sheen said. 'You did give us a key. We never used to have a key back home.'

'I'm going to bed.'

'Do you want a drink before you go, Tina? Or to take up with you?' he asked.

'No, ta.'

'Goodnight then, love.'

'Goodnight.'

I had a quick wash and changed into my pyjamas. Then I got into bed.

In the darkness I listened to my own breathing. You know, I really concentrated on that for a while. My own breathing. Tina Rudy. Tina Rudy. Tina Rudy breathing. Then I listened to the silence of the house. And it wasn't just the silence which made me wonder but that it was a different kind of silence from any I'd experienced before. It was a loose kind of silence. Not a tight one. Like a loose and easy-fitting jumper, just a bit too big to make it extra comfortable. To make movement easier. There was no tension. Nothing in the silence which made my adrenalin burn. Just the silence, that was all. A peaceful kind of silence. A sleeping house, I thought. A real sleeping house. Then I thought of Jilly. Her bedroom was next to ours. I wondered if she was asleep. Then I thought of Daniel and Rebecca. I wondered about Rebecca being in the pub. Then I thought of what Jilly had told me about her knowing lots of people who got into trouble with the police and her running that centre. Perhaps that was why she was friends with that hard guy in the pub. But fancy him being friends with a girl like Rebecca. I mean, I bet she never had any fights or got into trouble. I was sure Jilly would have told me if she had. Crumbs, it was right confusing thinking about Rebecca.

Oh well, what the hell.

I closed my eyes and when Sheena came in I pretended to be asleep.

Me and Sheen didn't wake up until ten thirty the next morning. Then, when we woke we stayed lying in bed until quarter past eleven. Just chatting about stupid things, we were. Joking. Larking. Tra la la.

There was no one in the house when we went downstairs. In fact, after we had breakfast I thought Sheen might have suggested us going through the place again. But she didn't.

'You know what?' she said, when we were having a fag and a cup of coffee. 'You know what that Rebecca does?'

'What she does?'

'Yeah.'

'She runs a centre or something.'

'Who told you?'

'Jilly.'

'And you never told me?'

I shrugged.

'That's why she was in the pub last night. She reckons she's mates with all of them, yer know.'

'Yeah.'

'She reckons she's mates with them. Would you believe that?'

'Perhaps she is mates with them. She looked it.'

'It's a real weird situation if you ask me anything.'

'Why?' Although I knew partly what Sheena meant. Because of what I'd been wondering about Rebecca myself. It just interested me more than anything. But I don't think Sheen was just interested in the same way as I was.

'I reckon she must have her hooks over them or something,' she said.

'What?'

'Why else would they want anything to do with her?'

'Perhaps she helps them by running this centre.'

'Crap.' Sheen twisted the last inch of her fag so that the burning piece of ash fell in the ashtray.

'No one helps anyone else without some ulterior motive.'

Sheena really frustrated me sometimes. Because she just couldn't see any further than she wanted to see. 'That's what I've been trying to tell you,' I ran my hands through my hair. 'It's different here. That's what I said yesterday. It's different here. You made out we'd just be the same, but you didn't know it would be different. Uncle Howard's a vicar. You said he's a walkover. Why's he a walkover?'

'Shit, you don't half complicate matters sometimes. You think too much, that's your trouble. All I'm saying is, she's hiking them and she's doing it so well that they're falling for it.'

'Maybe she's just a good person.'

'OK. If you say she's a good person, perhaps she is, but she's still hiking them. We wouldn't stand for a soft head like that in our crowd.'

'You liked her when you saw her motorbike.'

'Yeah, I bet that's how she's hiking them. Getting all the stuff, see. Making an impression. I'll tell yer something, though. It ain't gonna work with me.'

I sighed.

'And what the hell are you sighing for?'

'Nothing.' Fear of her leapt into my heart. Again. 'Nothing. Honest. You're right. OK? OK, you're right.'

'The day we start taking notice of cows like her is the day we wave the pigging white flag. And the only thing that means is surrender. And we're the ones that have to surrender. Not the likes of her. They'll sit pretty, like they've always sat pretty. They'll always try and rob us, though. Rob us to shit on us. That's how it goes. If we let it.'

I listened to her. And her words began to stir up an anger in me. Because it was true what she said. It's like there are two sorts of people. The good guys and the bad guys. But it's always the good guys who come out top in everything. The good guys who've always had everything. Easy. Easy. Easy. It's all been so easy for them. Then, perhaps they come along to try and help us. But help us for what? Help us to be shat upon again and again. Hell, Sheen was right.

'Are we gonna do anything then?' I asked her. Feeling stirred up for action. Any action.

'We're gonna bust up her little party, that's what we're gonna do.'

'Bust it up?' It sounded good.

'Yeah. Bust it up.' Her eyes gleamed.

'Rudy. Rudy. Rudy,' I chanted.

'Oi. Oi. Oi.'

'Rudy.'

'Oi.'

'Rudy.'
'Oi.'
'Rudy.'
'Oi.'
'Rudy.'
'We're gonna bust up her party.'
'Oi. Oi. Oi.'
'Rudy.'
'Oi.'
'Rudy rules.'
'Oi. Oi. Oi.'
'And we ain't never gonna surrender.'
'Oi. Oi. Oi.'
'We're gonna bust up her party,' Sheen repeated.
'Yeah.'
We shook on it.

Chapter 8

A few days later we went to that centre. In the village hall.

There was someone sitting at a desk, just inside the double swing doors. A woman. She smiled at us when we went in.

'Hello,' she said. 'Are you new?'

'Actually we're Rebecca Holdaway's cousins,' Sheen said. 'We thought we'd just come to have a look around like.'

'Oh yes. Tina and Sheena, isn't it? Rebecca was telling us about you coming to live with them. Well, welcome in. Have a look around by all means. We have different activities each day. We've got boxing today for the boys and weight-training for the girls. That's in the main hall, straight through there. I expect that will interest you a bit more than what the older of us do.'

'Oh, we're interested in everything,' Sheen said. Sounding real friendly-like. Her tactic for the day. 'Yeah, we're real interested in everything.'

'Well, in that smaller room there we have some of us teaching the younger people who can't read and write very well. And who have difficulty in adding and subtracting. They teach on a one to one basis, which we find works much better for the pupil. Then we have a jobs advice centre where a professional person comes in three times a week to advise everyone on jobs.'

The woman sounded as if she would ramble on for

hours. I was getting bored with it, so I nudged Sheen and she took the hint.

'We're just gonna have a look around then,' she said.

'By all means. Rebecca is about somewhere. I expect you'll come across her.'

We escaped from the lady and pushed our way through some more swing doors to the large hall. There was a buzz of heightened activity going on and I felt a bit deflated. Suddenly. When no one seemed to take any notice of us two. They were all so engrossed in what they were doing.

What were they doing?

Well, the hall seemed to be divided into two. I was more interested in the boxing ring and the punch-bags on the right-hand side. There were loads of guys. All in sports gear. Shorts and vests. Boxers' gear, yer know. There must have been about twenty in all. Some of them were skipping with ropes. Some of them were prone on the floor doing exercises. Then two of them were firing punches into two punch bags. There were two men in tracksuits. One was in the ring with a guy. And the man had a sort of giant pad thing attached to his hand and he was dancing round with the boy and the boy kept firing punches into it.

'Recognize any of them?' Sheen asked.

I hadn't really thought. 'Don't know.'

'I do. From down the pub.'

On the left-hand side of the hall was a group of girls in a large circle holding weights. There was also a man there in a tracksuit who looked to be in charge of them. He turned a tape recorder on and all the girls watched him as they started doing exercises with the weights. Up. Down. Behind their backs. On their necks. In time to the music.

I preferred the boxing.

So did Sheen.

We walked over to be nearer the ring. In doing so I tried to look for anyone I recognized from the pub. And when I passed them I noticed two guys doing sit-ups. They were the ones in suits who'd been playing snooker.

Sheen leant against the boxing-ring ropes, so I did the same.

'Left hook,' the man was saying. 'Left hook. Jab. Jab. Jab. That's it. That's it. Now move. Keep yer guard up. Move. Use yer feet. Use yer feet. Jab. Jab.' The guys in the ring were really dripping with sweat. Flying off them, it was.

'OK. That's enough,' the man said, ruffling the boy's hair. 'That's enough, Alan. Have a rest. Good boy. Jabs coming along lovely.'

'Ta, George,' the boy said before climbing out of the ring.

'Johnny. Let's have you up here.' The man beckoned to a guy who was sitting on a bench doing nothing. 'Come on, Johnny. We haven't got all day.'

'Sorry, George. Give us a chance.' The boy was thin and wily-looking. He had jet-black hair and looked Italian like. George cuffed him round the ear when he finally got in the ring. It was just a friendly cuff, yer know, but I could sense that it disgusted Sheen. 'Cos she moved away from the ring then and I followed her. We walked to a hatchway, which must have been for serving refreshments because it led into the kitchen. But there was no one in the kitchen then so me and Sheen just leant against it and lit fags.

'Some place,' Sheen mumbled.

'Yeah.' It struck me, though, the centre. Yer know. I never realized so much would be happening and it wasn't all stupid, boring things either. As I'd thought it would be.

'Some place,' she repeated.

'I don't see Rebecca around anywhere.'

'Her set-up.'

'What?'

'This. Her set-up.'

'Yeah.' I knew what Sheen was thinking. About busting up Rebecca's party and all that. Well, yer know, me too. I'd been ready for action. All set up like. But coming into the place, well, it all seemed so organized and fixed. Everyone seemed to be in their place. And me and Sheen, no one had bothered about us. Well, I got to thinking then, what could we do? Bust up the party? Yeah. If it was just a party. But I could see this set-up wasn't so light and simple. It was something more fixed. Deeper. And there was some sort of atmosphere about it. Controlled. Not like the atmosphere in the pub when me and Sheen had walked in. Not like that at all. This place was different.

'We've got to work out a plan,' Sheen said to me. Later. In the afternoon. After we'd gone for a burn up and stopped in some woods. Way out in the country somewhere. Away from all civilization. 'We've got to work out a plan.' We were sitting sideways on our bikes. The sun was shining. 'Work one out to bust the party.'

'Maybe it ain't such a good idea.' I was risking it. But I didn't want Sheena to get into anything she couldn't get out of. And that concern outweighed my fear of her. 'Maybe we should leave it. We don't have to have nothing to do with her, do we?'

'We got to bust the party. OK?' she said. Real serious. Which didn't leave room for any more questioning.

'OK.'

'And we got to work out a plan.'

'OK.' Again.

'So get yer thinking cap on.'

'It ain't gonna be easy.'

'We could just set fire to the joint.'

'Yeah, and get put away for it.'

'Or we could do it more subtle.'

'More subtle?'

'Like take some of our crowd down there. Then they'll do what we say and not what she says.'

'Or we could just try and get in there with them and gradually pull them away.'

'Or we could be even more subtle.'

'How?'

'Frame-up job.'

'What?'

'Frame-up job.' She smiled.

But I didn't quite understand.

'Work out who's one of the top guys in there. Do a frame-up job on him and then on Rebecca. When the kids find out, we can get in there and stir them all up. That simple.'

'Yeah?'

'Well, don't sound quite so enthusiastic.'

'We ain't never done anything like that before, though.'

'First time. Lucky time. We've gotta learn about bigger stuff, yer know. Stealing's, stealing, ain't it?

Taking stuff to Billy and all that. But some time we gotta make the decision to go up. 'Cos we can go up. We got what it takes, yer know.'

'Yeah?'

'Yeah! I ain't kidding. We ain't got nothing round our necks now. We can just do what the hell we like. We're free. We were free as soon as that bastard got sentenced.'

I didn't like it, though. Hell, something was nagging at the back of my mind and I didn't know what it was. Tick. Tock. Tick. Tock. Like a clock. A clock telling me the time. Trying to tell me. But Sheen was there. Still there. As she always was there. All the time. Still the same. I didn't know what was wrong with me. In the past Sheen's ideas had always been first class by me. Real first class. Real tops. In the past. What's changed? Nothing's changed. Hell, nothing's changed. Has it?

'What we doing now?' I asked her.

'Going over Jonny's.'

'I ain't.' Not with my eye still blackened.

'Say yer come off yer bike.'

'No. They'll know.'

'Well, I'm going.'

'OK, you go.'

So we stayed with each other all the way back until Sheen went straight on at a roundabout and I turned right. Turned right to go towards Lower Radford.

As I walked to the back door of the vicarage I saw Uncle Howard sitting in his study, which faces on to the back lawn. He was on the phone but smiled at me. I nodded my head to him.

I let myself in. Then I took off my crash helmet and jacket and went into the kitchen. I put on the kettle, then I wondered if Uncle Howard would like a cup of something. But, yer know, I suddenly felt real nervous-like to go and ask him. I don't know why. I was just scared to ask him if he wanted a cup of tea or coffee. Anyway, he made it easier then because he came into the kitchen. In his dog-collar he was. Brown cotton trousers. He always wore brown cotton trousers. Every day. It drove me crazy. Made me laugh inside.

'Hello, Tina,' he said.

'Hi.'

'All right?'

'Yeah.'

He yawned then.

'D'you want a cup of coffee?' I asked. Quickly. Before I had a chance not to ask.

'Coffee? Yes please. I've got to go out in half an hour, so that'll just do nicely.' Uncle Howard sat on one of the kitchen stools and read through a letter which had been lying on the kitchen table.

I made the coffee.

'D'you take sugar?'

'Two, please.'

'D'you have milk in your coffee?'

'Just a touch, love.'

I thought it looked pretty foul, the coffee I'd made, but he never told me it was rubbish, so it must have been OK.

I wasn't sure then whether he wanted me to stay in the kitchen or go out and leave him alone. So I was just standing there, dithering.

'Sit down, Tina,' he said.

So I sat. Feeling kind of awkward. Nervous, you know. And I had that sickness surge in my stomach again.

'About dinner, Tina.'

'Yeah.'

'Now you've settled in a bit we'll go back to having dinner in the evening at six. We have it together. When Rebecca is staying here she cooks it. But when she's not, Daniel and I sort of bustle together. And Jilly helps when she's not feeling awkward. Her job's to lay the table but it doesn't always get done.'

I nodded.

'So, if you can be ready for about six o'clock. That would work out nicely.'

'OK, I'll tell Sheen.' But I didn't know what her reaction would be. When we were living at home, if we were just one minute late we'd get a belting and then our meal would get chucked away. So we really had to be on time. But now, Sheena reckoned herself to be so free, I doubted that she'd want to be tied down to any times. But it didn't bother me.

'What d'you do with all your time, Tina? Every day. What d'you get up to?'

I shrugged. Tensing. 'Not much. Ride about. See our mates.'

'In Sugbridge?'

'Yep.' I hate being asked questions. That was Dad's favourite game when he was getting at us.

'D'you get bored?'

'If we get bored we fight.' I smiled at him then. Kind of winding him up, I was trying to. But it didn't seem to work with him. He just smiled as well.

'Ladies don't fight, do they?'

'We ain't ladies, are we?'

'What are you, then?'

He had me. It's the way he sort of looked at me With those eyes of his: 'What are you, then?' Smiling eyes.

As if they were looking right inside. Right inside me. As if they could see everything.

'This coffee's shit,' I said.

'Mine was all right.'

'I don't like this type of coffee. It's shit.'

'Maybe next time we go shopping you can come and choose a brand you like.'

'I hate shopping.'

'Right. I've got to go and get a few things together. Don't forget to make sure the back door's locked if you go out again. See you later.' He disappeared. Suddenly. In a flash. I thought he'd sort of got a bit angry then. The way he suddenly got up like that.

I sighed. It felt a bit flat then, after he'd gone. He was quite an interesting sort of bloke really. Different. That's what I'd say. Real different. To anyone I'd ever met before. Anyway, I felt bored then. I wished I'd gone with Sheena after all. But there was my eye to think about. There was my eye to think about. To think about.

Tra la la.

Bloody hell, I felt lousy. I had to write something. So I went upstairs. Sat on the bed with my notepad.

I am two, I wrote,
Trying to fit in one shoe,
The house is the shoe,
And I am two,
Sheen and me,
Have always been one,
Drinking tea,
And finding the sun,
I like to fight,
I like to steal,
I think it's like,

Going round in a big wheel,
Round and round,
Round and round,
Never stopping,
Never dropping.

I sighed. Stopped writing. Lay back on my bed. Looking at the ceiling. There was a yellow stain on the ceiling. Just by the lampshade. A yellow stain.

I wished Micky was around then. I felt like talking to him. Asking him what he really meant when he was getting all emotional with us. Take this chance. Take this chance. Oh yeah, it was easy for Micky. Easy for Micky to talk. Just words, they were. Easy words. And Sheen was right, yer know. Right when she said about the bad guys always getting shat upon. Because it was the truth. And that made me angry.

Who did the vicar think he was anyway? Taking us in. Being all nice. It was all a lot of crap.

And what about Rebecca? What about Rebecca? What an arsehole. Sheen was right. Again. She was right. We had to spoil the party. Do it right, yeah. Show them all that Rebecca was just a punk do-gooder. A punk do-gooder.

Chapter 9

I walked down to the village hall. Across the green from The Hatchet. I swung open the doors. Taking no notice of the lady sitting at the desk. There was music coming from the main hall. I walked straight through. The rock and roll music really hit me then. It was loud, yer know, real loud. And the whole atmosphere sort of knocked me out. There were guys dancing. Girls dancing. In the hall. They were all going crazy. Real dancing. Rock and rolling. Guys in leather jackets. Some dancing just with jeans on and no tops. Really sweating they were. I didn't understand what was happening. It was all pigging crazy.

There were a group of adults standing by the hatchway. They were talking and watching the dancing. Then I froze, 'cos I noticed him there. That guy in the pub. The hardest guy, with the scar running down his cheek. He was standing there in the group of adults and Rebecca was there as well. Rebecca was there. And then, just as I noticed her, she noticed me. And I couldn't do anything about her walking over to me.

'Hello, Tina,' she said.

'Hi.'

'You decided to come and have another look?'

I shrugged.

'It's dancing day on Tuesday.'

I didn't answer.

'Come on, I'll introduce you to a few people. If I can get them off the floor.'

I followed her round the side of the dance floor, and then waited while she went in amongst the dancers and nudged a couple of blokes and a girl. She beckoned them off the floor.

'I want you to meet Tina,' she said. Bringing them over. 'My cousin. Tina, this is Paul.'

'Hello, Tina.' He had cropped hair, blue eyes. He held out his hand. We shook.

'This is Gary.'

'Hi.' Gary had curly dark hair and a moustache.

'And this is Linda.'

'Pleased to meet you,' Linda shouted above the music.

'Hello,' I said.

'D'you want a cup of coffee or a Coke or something?' she yelled in my ear. 'I'll show you the kitchen. I'm ready for a break.'

'OK.' I didn't know what else to say.

'You two coming?' She turned to Paul and Gary. 'Drinks?'

They came too. Then Rebecca left us. We went through to the kitchen where it was a bit quieter.

I lit a fag.

'That's an hour non-stop.' Linda spoke. It seemed to no one in particular.

'Reckon they're watching Tim, yer know.' Paul took a Coke from the large fridge.

'They're watching everyone,' Linda said. 'That's what Rebecca reckons.'

'Will they take us on, though?' Gary sat on the table. His tee-shirt was wet with sweat.

'They might train us.'

'Not all of us.'
'About ten, maybe.'
'You'll get in, Linda.'
'Doubt it.'
'It's not only about rock and roll, yer know. You're great at the funk stuff.' Gary demonstrated what he meant.
'We'll just have to wait and see. What d'you want, Tina? A cold drink or coffee?'
'I'll have a Coke.'
She handed me one.
'Ta.'
'Sit down,' she said.
I sat on one of the stools.
'Is this your first time here?'
'I had a quick look the other day.'
'It's all happening today,' Gary said. 'You picked the right day to come.'
'Can yer dance?' Paul asked.
'Yeah.' I'm pretty good at dancing actually.
'Well, you should get out there later. We've got top nobs from London down here. They're looking for people with talent at dancing.'
'Yeah?'
'Yeah. They're looking for people to form a dance group, like that of the Hot Gossip, yer know. They're looking for people they can train. And it doesn't matter if you're not real good at it already. They want to train those who otherwise wouldn't get the chance to do it.'
'So fame's the name of the game.' Gary waved his hands in the air.
'Why do they come here, though?' I wanted to know. It all seemed pretty far-fetched to me.

'Some adults out there want to give the unemployed a chance,' Linda said.

'This place is getting to be pretty famous now. Hot stuff.' Gary.

'How's that?'

Gary shrugged. 'We've got a lot of people here who've been in trouble with the Law. Well, they're still on the fringes, yer know. Rebecca is trying to get them to go straight. And there's this guy, Dave, who's just come out of prison.'

'He's got a scar down his cheek, that's how you'll recognize him,' Linda said.

I knew who they were talking about. Instantly.

'He had a daughter, Jane. She used to get into trouble and that. She was a right tough nut. Well, Rebecca befriended her, yer know. Becky just went into the pub where all the tough nuts hang out and started talking to them. And her and Jane got really friendly. And Jane even started going to church. And that's when Jane met Howard. And she got to thinking of him like a father. And it was all real cosy for a while like. But then for no reason Jane tried to set fire to the church. Just like that. It was lucky 'cos the fire never caught hold properly and only a bit of damage was done. Anyway, Howard got a bit angry about it but he forgave her. But she thought the other people at church were against her. Especially one bloke. So one day she did something to this man's car and he had an accident in it. He wasn't hurt but a young kid in the other car involved was killed.'

'So then the cops were after her,' Gary continued. 'But before they had a chance to get to her she'd written a letter to Howard and Becky telling them that she loved them but she couldn't cope with it any more.

And then she went off. She just disappeared. She was found in Dover. Dead. She threw herself off a cliff.'

Silence filled the kitchen. Just the sound of the music filtering in from the hall.

'She'd also written a letter to her father. Telling him all about Howard and Becky and about the centre. So when Dave was released from prison he came and found Rebecca, and he offered to help her, with the kids and that. Apparently Jane had told him in her letter that all she ever wanted to do was to go straight. And she could have gone straight but she didn't have the guts. Anyway, there was a big write-up in a national paper about the whole story. And Rebecca wrote about the centre and what she was trying to do. And after that a lot of people rang up and offered help. Loads of people came down here. Important people, yer know. They came down to see what was happening, and since then we've sort of taken off. Ain't we?'

'Yeah.' Linda and Gary together.

'We're gonna be on telly as well,' Paul said. 'In about a month's time.'

'So it's all a groove like,' Gary said.

'And there's me gone and landed myself a bleeding job,' Paul said. 'But I'm gonna keep up with me boxing. After work, I'm gonna keep up with that.'

I listened to it all. The story about Jane, Howard, Dave. I listened to it all. A story. A happening. Fact. Fact. And the facts spun around in my brain, trying hard to catch hold, so that I could make some sense out of them. So that my emotions would calm down and not be left hanging in mid-air as they were doing.

'Are you going to dance?' Linda asked me.

'I got a twin sister. She's real good at dancing.'

'Yumight as well have a go,' Gary said. 'You ain't got nothing to lose.'

I shrugged. What the hell anyway? I'll show them, I thought. I'll show them how Tina Rudy can dance.

The records had changed when we went back in. It was the Police on then. I like the Police, though. It was good music. A good beat. I took off my leather jacket and flung it on the floor. I sort of get psyched up to music. It gets right into my heart like. It takes me away somewhere.

Anyway, I'd just got on the dance floor and was warming up. You know, not doing anything too strenuous to begin with – when suddenly there was a great bang. Girls screamed and I turned round quickly to see what had caused it. Something had come flying through the window. And then, before anyone had the chance to do anything, there were another two crashes and another two windows were smashed.

Everything was in turmoil for a few minutes. Boys began to rush outside. Some other people had been cut by the glass and one guy was stretched out on the floor. His head was bleeding. I ran outside too. Just to see what was happening. There was nothing outside. Just a crowd of boys. But I'd heard the motorbike. I knew the sound of Sheen's motorbike. And I heard it in the distance. What the hell, I thought. What the hell?

'Who done it, Terry?' one of the boys asked another.

'I don't know. They're on bikes, though.'

'Was it any of our lot?'

'How the hell should I know?'

'Dave did Johnny over the other day.'

'It wouldn't be Johnny. Not after Dave done him over, you silly idiot.'

'OK, boys, come back inside, there's clearing up to do.' Scarred Dave came out then and gave an order. The boys obeyed. I didn't, though. I just stood there.

'You know anything about this?' he said to me. Just like that.

'What?' He real scared me. He reminded me of Dad so much, the way he spoke.

'You know anything about this?'

'No.'

'D'you know who it might have been?'

I looked at the pavement. 'No.'

'I don't believe you, honey.'

I didn't answer.

'You ain't as tough as your sister, are yer?'

I said nothing.

'Answer me when I ask you something. You ain't as tough as your sister, are you?'

'No.'

'So I'd advise you not to start playing around with this place. We don't have room for no stirrers in here. I deal with them, see. Good and proper. So you'd better tell your sister that. If she's got any ideas in her head she'd better get them right out again. And I'll tell you something else. Your old man might have laid into you but if I lay into you it'll be a damn sight harder than he did. Howard's a good man. Rebecca is a good woman. Don't muck them about. Because if you do, you'll end up losing.'

He walked back into the hall then and I just stood there. Feeling a class one idiot. Glad he'd gone, anyway. I believed him, yer know. What he said, he'd do.

Chapter 10

I walked back to the vicarage. Feeling shaken. Sheen had thrown those bricks through the windows. And she must have had some guys from Jonny's as well. But what was she doing? Hell, what was she doing? Just when you thought Sheen was on to one track she'd start walking a completely different one.

I sat in the lounge and felt really depressed. My mind was in a turmoil. I felt I was cracking up. Everything seemed to be going so fast. Moving. Just moving. And I couldn't hold it. Couldn't control the movement.

The lounge door opened. Daniel came in. He was dressed in shorts and a tee-shirt.

'Hello, Tina. Thought I heard someone come in.'

'Hello.'

'OK?'

I shrugged.

'Where've you been?'

'Over the centre.'

'Dance day, isn't it?'

'Yeah.'

'You had a go?'

'No. There's trouble over there.'

'Trouble?'

'Windows smashed.'

He whistled. 'Wow-ee. Wow-ee. What a life.' He dropped down on to the settee. 'What a life.' But he didn't seem perturbed. Not by life. Not by anything. 'You're into crime, aren't you?' he said.

It was strange, the way he said it. Matter of factly. You're into crime, aren't you?

'Yeah.'

'So you stole a cross and a pen. From my room.'

I looked at him.

'You're lucky. Dad's giving you this one chance. He's buying me another cross and pen. He's giving you this one chance. He won't do it again, though.'

I said nothing.

'And who broke my radio?'

I looked down at my hands. Fingers. Twisting. Twisting.

'That was the last present my gran bought me. It was a sick thing to do.'

I smiled. It was the only thing, it seemed, to do.

'I reckon it was Sheena, anyway. She's the hard case.'

'I broke it.'

'You never.'

'I broke it.' I stared at him.

He laughed.

'Piss off,' I said.

'No.' He looked back at me.

'I'll bust yer.'

'Go on then. Bust me. I won't stop you.'

I took out my flick knife. Brought out the blade. He was scared then. I could tell by his eyes that he was scared. But he just sat there. He didn't try running or anything.

'D'you like scaring people?' His voice trembled. Slightly.

'Yeah, I love it.'

'Why?'

'Because I do.'

'So, you've scared me. You've won, OK?'

'What's going on?' Uncle Howard was standing there. In the doorway. Looking at my flick knife.

'What's going on, Daniel?'

'Nothing, Dad.'

'What's the knife for, Tina?'

'Busting up your son.' I stared at him.

'Has Daniel upset you, Tina?'

'Why don't you just piss off, Mr Pussy Eyes?'

'Daniel, I'll talk to you later. Will you leave us, please.'

He left. Pussy eyes closed the door.

'Give me the knife, Tina.'

'No.'

'Give me the knife.'

'Piss off. I'll give it to yer. In the guts. That's what I'll do.'

'Is that what you want to do?'

'I wanna piss off out of this place, that's what I want to do.'

'You're a free agent. You can go if you want to go.' He sat on the settee.

'I ain't got nowhere to go. That's why I'm staying here. I ain't got nowhere to go.' It wasn't the truth, of course. Not really. But I wasn't going to tell him the truth. I wasn't going to tell anyone the truth. Because the truth was way down deep inside me somewhere. Way down deep. And sometimes it was so deep that it was hidden from me.

We sat in silence. I fiddled with my flick knife. And felt conscious of his eyes. Looking at me. Studying me. Penetrating. I felt conscious of his presence. It made me tense. It made me alive. And it did something else to me. Something else which I didn't quite understand.

The clock ticked on. And we stayed there. I could have walked out. Left him. I could have given up. Given up. It was like a fight, sort of. Us two sitting there. A fight. Two boxers. Jab. Jab. Hook. Upper cut. Pow. Pow. Pow.

A mental fight. Done in silence. With no one else watching. Just us two. No one else.

'Are you going to carry on fighting for the rest of your life?' he asked.

The bell rang. End of round one. Seconds in the corner. Gumshields out. Sponge on face. Hands on head.

'Tina?'

Pow. Pow. Pow.

'There's no reason for you to fight now. No reason.'

'There is a reason.' Because the bell had rung again. Seconds out. Stool out. Round two.

'What is it?'

'Everyone else fights.'

Pow. Guts. In the guts. Winded. Winded. All of a sudden. No air.

'Not everyone, Tina.'

Air. Breathing for air. Wanted to get out of the ring. Outside. Away from the fight. But I was tough. I was hard. I could make it. I could win. I had to stay.

'Everyone fights.'

'But that's not the real reason, is it, Tina? Why you fight. Not physically. I mean mentally.'

The sweat. Pouring off my body. The smell of leather. The smell of blood. My blood. I was getting hit. Harder and harder. All the time.

'Why don't you talk about it?'

'Nothing to talk about.'

You can't talk. Not in the ring. You just have to keep on standing. Someway.

'I'll win,' I said.

'Who are you fighting?'

'I'll win,' I said.

'When will you win?'

End of round two.

'When I win. I'll win.'

'Do you want to win?'

'I want to die.'

That was it. The last punch. I was knocked out. Falling to the ground. Cold. Down and down further. I started crying then. Bloody hell, it was crazy, me crying. But the tears came and wouldn't stop coming. Uncle Howard was there. Suddenly. His arm around me. His hand gently pressing my head against his shoulder. His face touching mine.

'It's all right,' he kept saying. 'It's all right. It's all right. It's all right.'

I cried until no more tears would come. Howard held me until I stopped crying. Then he took the knife from my hand and I let him.

'D'you fancy walking somewhere?' he asked.

'Walking?'

'Yeah. We could go along by the river. It's nice there. Peaceful.'

'All right.'

'I'll see if Daniel wants to come too.'

'D'you know there's trouble over the village? In the centre.'

'Is there? What's happened?'

'Windows have been smashed.'

'We'd better pop in there first then. I'll go and get Daniel.'

Daniel and I went into the centre with Uncle Howard. The police had arrived by then. But apart from the police everything seemed back to normal. The dancing was going on again, anyway. Boards had been put over the broken windows. A policeman was talking to Rebecca and another man. We walked over to them.

'Hello, Howard,' the policeman said. 'Three smashed windows. A few cuts. A few bruises. A nice little note tied to one of the bricks.' The policeman held out a plastic bag to Uncle Howard with a piece of paper in it.

I looked at the paper over Uncle Howard's shoulder. The words were made of newspaper cuttings.

WE'RE OUT TO SCREW YOU.

They were the words. In untidy lines. We're out to screw you. That was all. I turned away from the words. Walked away from Uncle Howard. I watched the dancing.

'Hello, love,' the copper said to me.

I tensed. Immediately. Coppers had a smell, you know. A real smell. It made yer sweat.

'Hi,' I said.

'Tina Rudy, isn't it?'

Coppers always knew our name. No matter what part of the country we were in. Coppers always knew. Names get passed on, see. Between the coppers. Names stick like Sellotape. They always stick, no matter what.

'You know my name,' I said.

'Staying with your uncle, then?'

'That's right.'

'How's Sheena?'

'OK.'

'You've got a nasty eye.'

'Yeah. Come off me bike.'

'Where is Sheena then? You two stick together, don't you?'

'I don't know where she is.'

Uncle Howard was still talking to the other policeman. I wished he'd get a move on.

'When you see your sister, tell her we'll be calling to have a chat with her.'

'OK.'

'We're just going to give her a little warning, see? We don't want any trouble on our patch. And trouble seems to have a habit of following the Rudys around, doesn't it, love?'

I sniffed. Looked down at his polished black boots. Large feet. I wanted to kick him then. Kick him right between the legs.

'You all right, Tina?' Rebecca appeared. I could tell she sensed something was up between me and the copper. Because she eyed him, yer know. She eyed him as if she was on my side. That gave me confidence. 'He's just giving me a warning,' I said. 'Reckon he thinks I busted the window.'

'Now you're jumping to conclusions, love,' the copper said.

'She was in here when the windows were broken.' Rebecca.

'He probably won't believe yer.' I sniffed.

'I was asking her about her twin sister, actually.'

'Perhaps it would be better if you came round our house in future to ask questions. Then Tina wouldn't be on her own, would she?'

'Don't get uptight, Rebecca. You called for us.'

'No I didn't call for you. Someone else did. Someone who doesn't know me very well. Come on, Tina, let's get some fresh air.'

I went with Rebecca, outside.

'D'you want one?' She offered me a cigarette.

'Ta.'

'Was he giving you hassle?'

'Coppers all do. Rudy, see. They all know Rudy.'

'Yeah, well, that really bugs me when they start giving hassle. There's no reason for it.'

'They wanted to know about Sheena. They're going to see her.'

'Just as long as they come to the house.'

'Oh, they don't bother Sheena. She can deal with them.'

'Tina.'

'Yeah?'

'This window business and the note. You don't know anything about it, do you?'

'No.'

'What about Sheena?'

'She's gone down to Southend this afternoon with a few mates. It couldn't have been her.'

Rebecca smiled. 'That's OK, then.'

Yeah. That's OK.

Chapter 11

'Look, I can't come for a walk after all,' I said to Uncle Howard.

'Why not?'

'I've just remembered I've promised to meet this bloke. This afternoon. In half an hour. I just remembered.'

'OK then. You go off. You can walk with us another day.'

I sped over to Jonny's as fast as I could go. And real worried I was that Sheen wouldn't be there. But she was. Sitting in her place. Queen of her castle.

'Watcha, Teeny,' she said.

I sat next to her. And felt just a bit edgy. She looked so calm and relaxed, as if nothing had happened. As if there wasn't anything to worry about.

'Watcha, Teeny. Guess what we've been doing this afternoon.'

'I know what you've been doing this afternoon.'

'You do?'

'Yeah. I was in there at the time.'

'You were in there? Were yer? Hey, Terry,' she called across the café. 'Tina was in there this afternoon when we smashed the windows. What was it like, then? Was it OK, Tina? Good bleeding show, I reckon.'

'The cops are on to us. On to you. About this

afternoon. They were sniffing around. They're gonna come and see you.'

'Don't worry about the cops. We're all well and truly alibied for this afternoon. Terry's sister. We were in with her all afternoon. Her brother-in-law was there as well. So, we're clean, honey.'

'I told Rebecca you went down to Southend this afternoon.'

'What d'yer tell her that for? Why was she nosing? She's on to me too, is she? How did she like our little threat? Scare her, did it?'

'She was helping me. With the copper. She was sticking up for me.'

'That's how she does it, baby. Good girl, you're psyching her. That's what we need. Find her weak points.'

'Why d'yer do it this afternoon, though? Thought we were going to make a plan. Why d'yer do it?'

'Hey, man, you look as if you've been crying.' She held my chin, her eyes scrutinizing my face. 'You look as if you've been crying. What's been happening?'

'I ain't been crying. Just a fly or something got in me eye. On the way over here.' I'd never lied to Sheen before then. Never. Ever. She'd lied to me. But I hadn't to her. Never before.

'You have been crying,' she said.

'The coppers are gonna come to see you tonight.' I tried to change the subject. 'Round the vicarage.'

'Are you lying to me?'

'What?'

'You heard.'

'Look, I've got to get back. I only came to warn you about the coppers.'

'Why have you got to get back?'

'I'm going out, that's why. Out with Uncle Howard.' The words just came out. Quickly. And they had a sort of sting to them. I was surprised at hearing that sting. From my own lips. Against Sheena.

She laughed. 'You're going out with Uncle Howard?'

'Yeah.'

'Psyching them?'

I picked up my helmet. Stood. Ready to go. She grabbed hold of my arm. 'Psyching them?'

I just looked at her.

'You should be learning quite a bit by now,' she said. 'About the family. Got a lot to tell me. We'll talk tonight. Then we can work out some more moves, can't we?'

'Yeah.'

I wished I hadn't gone over, to warn her. All the while back to Lower Radford, I wished that. 'Cos she'd got everything sorted out herself. She didn't need me at all. And then she knew I'd lied to her. And she also knew I'd never lied to her before. But she knew. Just like that. She knew I'd been crying too. And it had got to her because of me crying. She knew something else too. Something else inside me which perhaps I didn't even know myself. You see, Sheena could sense things about me as if she was a radar or something. Feelings. About me. Sheena was clever like that. But it left me open to her. Left me open so that I could never hide anything. That's why I never let her see the notepad. Because that was my own. My very own. It had nothing to do with her. And she knew nothing about it. I could hide things in there. Hide anything I wanted. Hide my stories:

Once upon a time a girl wrote a rhyme. Turning it over in

her mind, hearing it like two stones that against each other grind. And upon the paper her pen moved swiftly, the words she used ever so thriftly. Because she knew not many. She was not bright. All she really liked to do was fight. All she really liked to do was fight.

Chapter 12

Sheen came bouncing into our bedroom. 'Hiya, honey-bun,' she said. It was six o'clock. 'Just in time for dinner. Uncle Howard said for me to tell you it's ready.'

'OK.' I threw my pillow at her then. Just to make sure things were back to normal between us. She chucked it back. Flinging herself on top of me as she did so.

'Hey, get off.' She was sitting on my head. 'Get off, you oaf.'

'Not until you tell me what you were crying for.' She grabbed my wrist and started twisting it. I tried to kick her in the head, but she ducked out of the way.

'Aaah, get off, Sheen. You've done me over once this week.'

'I'll break yer fingers.'

'Get off.'

'Tell me then.'

'OK. OK. But get off first. Get off.'

She got off. Just sitting on the bed. Then she ruffled my hair until it was all messed up. Then we just started laughing. We used to do that sometimes. Just laugh. For no reason, really. Well, for a stupid reason. Like Sheen pulling a face like a loony, which she did then. A real weird face. It made me curl up. After we'd stopped laughing, though, Sheen was serious again. 'What were you crying for?'

I shrugged. 'I don't know. Uncle Howard was talking to me. I just started crying.'

'Was that punk getting at yer?'

'No. Just talking.'

'Well, it's sure funny that just talking could make you bawl.'

'He was talking about why I had to fight all the time.'

'Hell. You know what he's trying to do, man. You know what? He's trying to psych you, when the hell it should be the other way round. That's all he's trying to do, Tina. Psych yer. He wants to get in control. And you fell for it.'

'I gave him my knife.'

'You what?'

'Gave him me knife. I had it out, see. I was gonna do Daniel. He was coming it, so I got my knife out. Then he came in.'

'You bloody idiot. You really crack up when I'm not around, don't yer? So he took yer knife?'

'First of all I told him he could have it in the guts.'

'Then you started crying. He came a bit softy and you let him have yer knife.'

'Yeah.' She was right again. As she usually was. But it made me feel stupid. How I'd acted with Uncle Howard. And how I'd given him my knife. Now it seemed stupid. Now, because I felt angry at letting myself go to Uncle Howard. You know, crying and all that. My stories are my stories, I figured out in my mind. Stories about happy families are just stories about happy families. Stories are stories are stories. But those stories didn't touch life. My life. The way it was. The way it had to be. They didn't touch my life at all.

'Come on, let's go down to dinner.' Sheena pulled me off the bed. 'We can talk afterwards. After the fun.' She winked and I knew what she meant. Fun. Have some fun at dinner. I rushed down the stairs after her.

Our dinner was on the table. All the others had started theirs already. They hadn't been eating for long, though.

We sat down. Not saying anything. Well, Sheen said nothing, so I copied her. I had a feeling that it was going to be her show. I just had to tag along in support. And doing that caused an awkward silence around the table. Real awkward, because we were playing it cool and hard. Getting back at Uncle Howard for trying to psych me.

'Who cooked the dinner tonight?' Sheen said, eventually.

'I helped cook it,' Jilly smiled.

'Is something wrong with it then, Sheena? I thought you told me you liked steak and kidney pie.' Uncle Howard.

'Is something wrong with it then, Sheena?' my twin mimicked, to me.

'It's shit,' I replied. 'I bet Rebecca cooked it. That's why it's shit.'

'Naughty, naughty.' Sheen wagged her finger. 'You mustn't swear at the vicar's table. He might smack your botty.'

Jilly giggled then. She was great, was Jilly.

'I don't want a smacked botty.' I carried on with the game. Aware of the looks circulating the table. 'Please don't give me a smacked botty, daddy.'

'If you kiss my feet I won't give you a smacked botty. You must kiss my feet first, though.'

'OK. You've had your fun, girls,' Uncle Howard

said; agitation showing in his pussy eyes. 'Now get on with your dinner.'

'What d'you think, Jilly?' Sheen asked. 'Do we have to do what the vicar says?'

Jilly looked at Uncle Howard, then at me. 'I don't like this dinner, Dad. It tastes all smelly.'

'How can a dinner taste smelly?' Rebecca tried to cool the situation a bit.

But Sheen was ready. Jumping in. Like Zebedee. 'Of course a dinner can taste smelly,' she said. 'This one does, so a dinner must be able to taste smelly.'

'See, I told you,' Jilly said. 'It's like dogs' stuff.'

I laughed at that.

'Jilly, if you don't like your dinner you'd better leave it and go up to your room,' Uncle Howard said. 'I'll talk to you later.'

'I don't want to go to my room. I can stay here.'

'That's it, stick up for your rights, girl.' Sheen pointed her knife at Jilly. 'Don't be trod upon.'

'Jilly, do as Dad says,' Rebecca intervened.

'Why?'

'You might get a smacked botty, otherwise,' I said. Nudging Sheen.

'Dad never hits us.' Daniel.

'He's a big softy,' Sheen said. 'As soft as . . .'

'This lump of meat.' I poked it. 'This lump of meat like dogs' stuff.'

'Jilly. I told you to go up to your bedroom.'

'What for?'

'I won't tell you again.'

'Why do I have to go up to my bedroom and not them two? They swore at the table.'

'We're special,' Sheen said. 'And the vicar knows we're special.'

Uncle Howard stood up and walked over to Jilly. Then he leant over her. Getting close, like. Real close. 'Do you want to break friends with me, Jilly? Because if we break friends there'll be no more ice-creams, no more comics, no more dancing lessons.'

'No more smacked botties,' Sheen chipped in. But Uncle Howard didn't take any notice of her.

'Are you going, Jilly? Or are we going to break friends?'

'I like the dinner really.'

'Just go upstairs.'

'Well, can I have it later, then? Will you keep it warm?'

'Just go up to your room.'

'All right.'

When Jilly had gone Uncle Howard sat down again and carried on with his dinner. I waited to see what Sheen would do next, 'cos I knew damn well that she'd do something. But she was quiet for a while. Quiet until she'd finished her dinner After that she burped real loud.

'Uncle Howard,' she said.

He looked at her.

'Uncle Howard, Tina would like her knife back. Wouldn't you, Tina?'

'Yeah.'

'So, if you'd kindly hand it over we'd be very happy.'

Rebecca sighed then. A real deep long sigh. 'I'd better put Jilly's dinner in the oven, Dad.'

'Thank you, love.'

So then there was just Daniel, Uncle Howard, me and Sheena left.

'Did you hear what I said, Uncle Howard?'

'Yes, I did, Sheena. But I happen to have got rid of the knife.'

'Well, I'd say that was a stupid thing to do, Mr Vicar.'

'Don't threaten my dad, Sheena,' Daniel said. Cool, like. Real cool he said it. 'He's not going to fight you, yer know.'

'You keep out of our affairs, Holdaway. This ain't got nothing to do with you.'

'Of course it's got something to do with me. This is my home.'

'This is my home,' Sheen mimicked, with hatred in her mimic. 'This is my home. This is my daddy. Why don't you grow up? Why don't you piss off?'

'Have we all finished dinner?' Uncle Howard said. 'If we have I'll go and get the pudding.'

'You shut up and listen to me,' Sheen snarled.

'Yeah, just listen,' I said.

'We could bust this place up, see? Just like that, if you don't listen. And you've got some lovely china about, haven't you?'

'Tina gave me the knife, Sheena. I didn't take it from her.'

'You psyched her, baby.'

'She gave me the knife.'

'Well, you shouldn't have got rid of it, see. That's all I'm saying. You shouldn't have got rid of it. But seeing that you did, you're going to have to pay for it.'

There was a ring at the door then. Breaking into everything Sheen had said.

'I'll go.' There was a shout from the hallway.

We all waited. It was as if we'd been caught in mid-air. Held in suspension.

Rebecca came into the dining-room. 'It's the police, Dad. To see Sheena.'

'All right, Sheena? You can take them into my study if you want. D'you want me there too?'

'I don't want you anywhere, darling,' Sheen said. Going out.

Rebecca breathed a sigh of relief when Sheen had gone. 'That was getting hot,' she said.

'Saved by the bell.'

'You're angry, aren't you?'

'Just a bit.'

'I told you it wasn't going to be easy, Dad.'

'It's not easy and I don't seem to be able to handle the situation very well either, do I?' Uncle Howard stood, slamming one plate on to the other. 'I'll go and get the pudding.'

'Pleased, then?' Rebecca spoke to me when he'd gone. 'Pleased, are you?'

'Yeah, that's right.' I smiled at her. I was pleased. I didn't care about Uncle Howard. I didn't care about the family. They were all poncy do-gooders. And they meant nothing to me, none of them did.

'Who are you trying to kid?' she said.

Which I couldn't think up an answer for. None came. Sheen would have thought of one but I couldn't.

'You just try and kid yourself, don't you, Tina? That you don't care. That nothing matters. You find something you need and then you pretend you don't want it.'

Psyching me, I thought. That's what Sheen said they were doing, psyching me. And I listened to Sheen. That's who I listened to. The only person. No one else. Not Rebecca Holdaway.

Uncle Howard came back with a bowl of rice pudding. Right stroppy he looked.

'Shall I go and see if Jilly wants some?' Daniel asked.

'No, leave her.'

Rebecca unstacked three pudding bowls.

'D'you want some rice, Tina?' Uncle Howard asked.

I didn't answer him. Just fiddled with the salt pot.

'Do you want some rice, Tina?'

I said nothing. And I didn't look at him but I was aware that he'd stopped dishing out the pudding.

'You either say yes or no.'

I looked at him then. Into his eyes.

'I didn't ask you to stare at me. I asked you whether you wanted any rice pudding. If you can't answer me you might as well get down from the table.' He was shouting then. Shouting.

I just sat there. Winning. I knew I was winning then. Because he was losing his cool.

'What d'you want me to do, Tina? Physically hit you? Will that make you move?'

I lurched inside then. Scared. A bit scared. But I knew he wasn't as tough as our old man. I knew he couldn't hit me that hard. So nothing else would hurt. So I just sat where I was. Silent.

'OK, I'll tell you something, Tina,' he said. 'I'll tell you something. I haven't wanted to tell you this because I didn't want you to have fear hanging round your neck. But you don't give me much choice. Every morning at some time I get a phone call from your brother. Only a very short phone call. Six words he uses. Six words. D'you want to know what they are?'

I'd frozen. My heart was the only organ in my body left moving. And that was pounding. Real hard it was pounding.

'Shall I tell you what his words are? Every day, the same. Shall I tell you?'

I didn't want to hear.

'"Are they causing you any trouble?" That's what he says. Are they causing you any trouble?'

But I had to hear. I had to hear. Because his voice was so strong.

'So, what sort of dilemma does that leave me in?' he continued. 'If I feel I can cope with you, I can say, I'm coping. But as soon as I feel I can't cope, what do I say to him then? And believe me, right now, I feel I can't cope. So what am I going to say to him tomorrow when he rings? I wonder to myself, is that what you want? Do you want someone to come and beat the living daylights out of you? Is that what you want, Tina? Because if it is I only have to give your brother the word. That's all I have to do. I can tell him tomorrow that you're too much to cope with. Then, maybe, you'll get what you want.'

'You don't have to tell him anything,' I said.

'But I do. Because this isn't working at the moment, is it?'

'I'll have some rice pudding then.'

'You should have said yes please, when I first asked. Not now. When you're under some sort of threat to eat it. I don't want you to be afraid. I don't want you to be afraid of getting beaten. That's not how our family works. That's not how it should work.'

'If you don't tell him anything, it'll be OK.'

'So now you're going to be straight, are you? In this house, with a threat over you, you're going to be straight?'

I began sweating. It was running down underneath my hair.

'I thought we were beginning to get on all right, Tina, me and you. But you suddenly change again, don't you? Suddenly take everything back to square one again. You can't keep trying. I know it's hard for you. It's not easy, but you've got to keep trying. Got to keep pushing. And most of all, you've got to find out what you want out of life. Who you want to be. What road you want to walk along. You've got to try and decide and make a move for that road before it's too late.'

'Can I have some rice pudding, please?'

He just looked at me a while. Before speaking. 'Yes, you may. We'll start again.'

He dished out a bowl of rice pudding then and handed it to me. Then he gave Daniel and Rebecca theirs. I didn't particularly feel like it, but I started eating.

'It looks as though our visitors are leaving,' Uncle Howard said, when we heard voices and heard the front door open.

I wondered if Sheen would come back in and begin where she left off, and I hoped she wouldn't. I really hoped like hell she wouldn't.

But she didn't. I heard her footsteps on the stairs and I was relieved inside.

I finished my rice and left the table. I went upstairs too. Glad to get out of that dining-room. But worried, real worried, about Micky.

'Bastard pigs,' Sheen said, outstretched on her bed. 'Bastard pigs.'

'Sheen, we can't muck him about.'

'They tried roughing it, yer know. Tried roughing it. Threats. Like hell, I was real shaking.'

'Sheen, listen. We can't muck Uncle Howard about any more.'

'What the hell are you talking about? Don't you care about me getting a toe-the-line job by the fuzz?'

'Micky rings him. Uncle Howard. Every day. He rings him. To make sure we're not causing any trouble.'

'Micky what? Speak slower. Don't gabble.'

'Micky rings Uncle Howard every day to make sure we're not causing any trouble. And Uncle Howard reckons he might tell him we have been causing trouble. So Micky would come back, after us, Sheen. He'd come back after us.'

'Don't talk crap.'

'It's the truth.'

Sheen smiled.

'It ain't nothing to smile about.'

'Poor Micky, he's really turning chicken, ain't he? Wanting us to keep on the straight and narrow. He's really turning chicken.'

'But it don't make no difference. He'll still come back after us.'

'OK, OK, don't panic.'

'So we got to cool it round here.'

'I have been cooling it round here. The only reason I laid into them tonight was because of you. I've been playing the good little niece all along. We don't need to hot things up round here anyway. As long as we stay in control. As long as we don't start letting them take us in, like you were doing.'

I sat on my bed. Sighed. It was all so simple, the way Sheena spoke. All so simple. She made it appear that way. And it was simple for her. But not for me.

'I can't just pretend all the time,' I said. 'Not like you do. I can't just pretend.'

'If you can't pretend, just keep out of their way. OK,

we have to sit with them at meal-times, but that's about all. Apart from that you can keep away from them. Easy. See?'

'Yeah, OK.' But I wasn't sure.

'Anyway, you're just going to have to, because if you don't I'm gonna get riled with them again and Micky will come running. If what you say is true.'

'It is true.'

'Well, then. You've got your answer.'

'Yeah.'

'Anyway, listen. Plans have been moving for busting up her party.'

I waited for Sheen to continue. I was prepared for anything since she broke the window.

'What we do,' she said, 'is do a frame-up job on Rebecca herself and the scarred fella. 'Cos I got Terry and Pete to go down their pub at lunch-time and find out more about him and Rebecca. The boys went in real friendly-like. Pretending they'd come from London and were looking for the unemployment centre. So they got talking to a few of them. And apparently that scarred bloke is the top guy in the centre. He helps out down there and roughs up anyone who causes trouble. Apparently he had a daughter who was mates with Rebecca or something.'

'Yeah, I've heard the story about his daughter. Today. When I was in there. She committed suicide.'

'Yeah. Anyway, all we needed to know was that he was the top guy.'

'His name's Dave.'

'So we frame Dave and Rebecca. They get done. We go in the centre and stir things up. You know, saying things like, they've been cheating on the kids, trying to make them go straight when they're into crime themselves, and all that. Then, hey presto.' She clapped her hands.

'Yeah, so how do we frame them?'

'Drugs.' Sheen's eyes were alight. 'We plant drugs on them. Then we give the police a tip-off and we're away.'

I s'pose it sounded quite a good idea in a way. Not too difficult, anyway.

'It'll be easier planting drugs on Rebecca. But Dave's got a car. We could shove them in there.'

'Great.'

'Good idea?'

'Where we getting the drugs from?'

'Jamie's getting hold of some for us. In a couple of days. He owes us anyway.'

I lay on my bed. Trying to get control of my feelings. Things were going so fast. My emotions were running. Just on. On and on. I couldn't get my breath. In danger of going under. Under somewhere. Down.

'Well?' Sheen said.

'Well.'

'Make some comment about my idea then.'

'Perhaps we should wait a bit. Perhaps it's too soon at the moment.'

'Too soon?'

'Yeah. Too soon,' I snapped at her.

'What the hell are you talking about?'

'I just said I think it's too soon,' I said, again.

'You think it's too soon,' she repeated, like a parrot, her voice incredulous. As if no one could disagree with her. How dare they?

'That's what I said.'

She laughed. A real nasty laugh. 'Goosing out, are yer?'

I would never have had the guts to go against Sheena before. Never had the strength. She knew everything. She was always right. But now I was beginning to wonder. And I was suddenly sick of being frightened of her all the time. And what we did at dinner. Well, I sort of felt ashamed about that. But I knew Sheena wasn't ashamed. I knew she could never be ashamed. That's what I knew about her.

'Yeah, perhaps I am goosing out,' I said. 'Perhaps I am.'

'You don't goose out of nothing,' she growled.

'Don't I? Who said?'

'I just said, see?'

'You don't own me.' I began to boil then. Anger, real deep anger at her, which had never come to the surface before. 'You don't own me, yer know.'

'Don't come it, Tina. Don't come it with me.' She pointed a finger at me. Then kicked at the dressing-table. Causing everything on top of it to go flying. 'Don't come it or you'll have a boot in yer crutch.'

'What d'you want me to do, then? Follow you around like a weak lamb all the time? Do exactly what you do?'

'I know your trouble. You've been listening to them down there too much. That's your trouble. And you were the one that said when we first came here that you were scared of changing. Well now, what the hell are you doing? Letting them down there walk all over yer. That's what you're doing.'

'That's what you say, they're walking all over me. Maybe they're not, though, maybe he's not. Uncle Howard. Maybe he just cares, that's all. Cares, you know. Or perhaps you've never heard of that word.'

'No one cares, darling. Not about the likes of us. Who

cares about shit? It just gets flushed down to the sewage, don't it? That's what happens to shit.'

'Well, perhaps, just perhaps, we ain't shit after all.'

'Oh God, now she's getting big-headed. Don't come above your station, darling. Or they'll only put you back down again. And it'll hurt more then. Much more. Stay where you are. You're sure to survive then.'

'Survive for what? To get put in the nick. For life. Like Dad is.'

'Haven't you forgotten about him yet?'

'He cracked up in court, didn't he? What's that supposed to mean? I can't just forget things, Sheena. I can't just forget what Micky said to us.'

'Micky's cracking up. That's what's wrong with him. Anyway, you were having a whale of a time down there tonight. Before those coppers came. We could have busted the place. We were really getting into the swing of things.'

'We upset him.'

'We what?'

'Upset Uncle Howard. He got angry.'

'Well, that's what the idea was, or didn't you realize?'

'I just don't want to upset him no more, that's all. He don't know how to cope, see. Because he's not like us. But he's trying to cope. He's trying for us. He's soft really, see? Too soft for us.'

'Not too soft to know about psyching.'

'See? You always get me riled up. Try to. I can't cope with my own feelings without you making things worse. OK, I felt angry with him. But I wouldn't have done all that tonight if it wasn't for you leading me on.'

'Oh, great. So it's you against me now then, is it? We're splitting, is that right?'

'I didn't say that.'

'I'm leading you on. You don't want me around. You want me to piss off. Why don't you say it, then? Have the guts to say it, baby face.'

I said nothing. Lay back on my bed. It was getting too steamy. I had to calm down. Had to stop spinning. Spin-ning.

'No, we ain't finished.' She yanked at me. 'We ain't finished with this yet.'

'I'm going downstairs.' I made for the door.

'Oh no you ain't.' She beat me to it. Stood against the door. 'Oh no you ain't, little girl. You're staying here. We're getting this thing sorted out.'

'There's nothing to sort out. I want to go downstairs.'

'I don't care what you want to do.' She shoved me. I fell back against the bed. 'You don't do what you want. You do what I want.'

'Look, piss off and let me go,' I yelled. 'I'm sick of your orders.'

'You go, but you got to get past this first.' Her flick knife was in her hand. The blade cutting into the air. Pointed at me. 'You go, but you got to get past this, darling.'

'You do something to me and he'll get Micky back here.'

'So he's on your side now, is he? Protecting you against me. Is that what it's all about?'

'He'll care for us both if we let him.'

'You reckon you can go straight? You're dreaming, girlie. You wouldn't be able to go straight even if you wanted to. It's in your blood, see. We've inherited it from our daddy, haven't we? You can't escape from it. You're what you are. If crime's in your blood it's in your blood. You can't escape, darling. You're stuck with it, whether you like it or not. You're stuck with it.'

Her words cut into me. As if they were that knife I felt powerless to defend myself. I had nothing to defend myself with.

'So you ain't chickening out of doing this job with me. We do it together. You plant drugs on Rebecca. I'll plant them on old scarface. That's how it's gonna work.'

I just sat there on the bed. Her words ringing in my head. Shit. Crime. No escape. Shit. Crime. No escape.

Drugs.

Rebecca.

'You can go down and play happy families to your heart's content, but you're doing that job. I promise you, you're doing that job. You got that?'

You got that? You got that? You got that? Echoing.

'Got it, darling? Yes or no?' She contorted her face. Right ugly, she looked.

'Yeah,' I said.

'You better have.'

'I've got it.'

'Now you can do what the hell you want and I won't cut yer. Piss off down there if you want.' It was her who pissed off, though. Slamming the door after her.

I just stayed where I was. It was weird. I'd never realized before how hateful Sheen could be. To me. She'd never been like that before. And I thought she cared about me. I really thought she cared about me. Getting beaten up by her was one thing, but being hateful like that was something completely different.

Chapter 13

I went downstairs. Into the lounge. Uncle Howard, Jilly and Daniel were in there. The telly was on. A quiz show or something. Jilly was sitting on Uncle Howard's lap. They were looking at a book together. Daniel was watching telly.

I just sat on the other end of the couch. Away from Uncle Howard and Jilly. Uncle Howard didn't look angry any more. He looked quite happy. He said nothing to me, though.

'We're getting a puppy,' Jilly said. 'Tina, we're getting a puppy.'

'Are yer?'

'Yeah. We're looking at all different sorts of dogs in this book. D'you want to see?'

I didn't know what to say really.

'Just because you're interested in dogs, Jilly, it doesn't mean that everyone else is,' Daniel said.

'Tina is interested, aren't you?'

'Yeah, I am.'

'Did you used to have a dog?'

'No.'

'Well, we'll soon have one, won't we, Dad?'

'After our summer holidays.'

'Yeah, after our summer holidays. But we'll probably only just get a mongrel puppy.'

'Has Sheena gone out, Tina?'

'Yeah.'

'Aren't you going?'
'No.'
'Ow, Jilly, sit still if you're going to . . .'
'I'm sitting still. I just got uncomfy just then.'
'Has Becky gone out, Dad?' Daniel asked.
My heart beat faster as Daniel used Rebecca's name.
'Yes.'
'Where's she gone?'
'To the pub, I expect.'
'She's always in that place.'
'Where's Sheena, Daddy?'
'Jilly!' Daniel exclaimed. 'You only asked that because I asked Dad where Becky was.'
'No I didn't, so there.'
'Yes, you did. You always have to copy. All the time.'
'Shut up.'
'Jilly!'
'Well, I don't always copy him. I wouldn't want to copy him anyway.'
'Either way, it doesn't matter, does it?'
'See, now she's forgotten all about asking where Sheena is,' Daniel said.
'Aaah, hard luck. I was just about to ask.'
'No you weren't.'
'Daniel, don't tease her. Why can't you two just do things quietly like Tina does?'
'Tina said her bit at dinner-time, didn't she?' Daniel mumbled.
I tensed inside then. But Uncle Howard winked at me. All nice-like. Back to being pussy eyes again. He winked at me, as if to say, don't worry.
'When did we last wash your hair, Jilly?' Uncle Howard fiddled with Jilly's hair.

'I can't remember.'

'She needs it washed again tonight,' Daniel said.

'It does look a bit greasy.'

'But we're going swimming at school tomorrow. So if you wash it tonight, it'll only get messed up again tomorrow.'

'Not if you wear your swimming cap.'

'Dad!' Jilly turned round so that her forehead was touching Uncle Howard's forehead. 'No one wears their swimming caps.'

'Don't they?'

'No.'

'All right. Tomorrow night we'll wash your hair.'

'Will you do it, Dad, instead of Rebecca? She gets loads of soap in my eyes.'

'If I'm in I'll do it. If not you can get Tina to do it,' Uncle Howard laughed.

'I can't wash your hair,' I said.

'I'll teach you tomorrow night,' Uncle Howard said.

'If you're in.' That was Daniel. 'If Dad's out, Tina, I'll teach you, instead.'

'I don't want Dan near my hair, Dad.'

'Whether you want Daniel near your hair or whether you don't is quite irrelevant, darling.'

'What?'

'Because if I'm not in he's going to teach Tina how to wash hair, OK?' He bit the end of her nose.

'Oh, OK.'

'Right, that's that sorted.'

The telephone started ringing then.

'I'll go, Dad,' Daniel said.

'No. I'll go. Off you get, Jilly.'

So Uncle Howard went out to answer the phone. Jilly began looking through the book again and Daniel switched over to watch Top of the Pops. I just sat back, my eyes on the telly, my ears listening to the music. But I wasn't really watching. I wasn't really listening. Everything was a blur. I was just thinking. Thinking about Sheen. About us falling out. About her gunning for me. Hating me. Yeah, that was it, she really hated me then. And I used to think she was the only one who would always be on my side. I realized then that she'd only be on my side if I agreed with her all the time. Went along with her. Which I always had done. Always. But now. Now. Now what? Am I changing? Do I want to go straight? Do I want to be the good girl of my dreams? Of my stories? Do I want to be? And what about Uncle Howard? What about the family? What do they stand for? What did they mean? Why had they suddenly come into my life so strongly? As if to knock all the stuffing out of me. All the stuffing which I thought was so strong and unbreakable. And why had I let them affect me when Sheena had just brushed them aside? And why did I care about Rebecca? Why didn't I want to do the job? I didn't want to frame her. I didn't want to. But I had to. Because of Sheen. My enemy now, when she used to be my only ally. She was making me do something I didn't want to do. But did I have a choice? Did I? Did I?

The music changed. A fast record. With a video on screen. Jilly began singing along. Daniel did too. Could I sing with them? Could I really belong? Did I want to? Would I ever if we did that job? Suddenly it was all too much. I couldn't stay in the lounge any longer. My body felt as if it was going to explode. So much going on inside. So much. So much. So much.

I dashed from the lounge. And out of the front door. Then once on the pavement I just ran. Ran. Ran. Ran.

On and on. Hearing my breath. Panting. Panting. But I still ran.

I ran along the road and back again. Back to the church. In front of me. It was a small church, but modern. The light of the day was gradually drawing in around it. Shadowing. Shadowing.

I don't know why I stopped running. I don't know why I opened the door of the church and went in. I don't know why. I didn't know why. I just did it.

The church was so quiet. The wooden seats were lined up like soldiers. Soldiers in silence, waiting for battle. I walked down the aisle. A wooden cross was in front of me. On the altar. I went up a couple of steps and held the wooden cross. It wasn't heavy really. I put it on the ground.

Then I went up some more steps to the pulpit. There was a large Bible there.

The door of the church opened. He was there. Pussy eyes.

'Get out!' I yelled.

'I've come to lock up.'

'Piss off.'

He walked up the aisle. Coming nearer me. Nearer.

'Piss off, I said.'

'Why did you run out, Tina?'

'Pussy eyes, that's all you are. Nothing but pussy eyes.'

'Is that my new nickname?' He smiled.

'Don't smile at me. Don't come it, OK? Just leave me alone.'

'You were OK ten minutes ago, what's upset you now?'

'You reckon I was OK ten minutes ago, do yer? Well, that's where you're wrong, honey. See, you don't know nothing.' I swung away from the pulpit. Down to the altar again. 'You don't know nothing.'

'Not if you don't tell me.'

'You're a vicar and you don't know sod all.'

'Then you've got to teach me, Tina.'

'Don't get any nearer, OK?' Because he was walking towards the altar.

'All right, I'll just sit here. This is my seat in church.'

'Church is a lot of crap.'

'Why?'

'Because you're the vicar and you don't know nothing.'

'What should I know, then?'

'Psych. Psych. Psych.'

'That's what Sheena says, isn't it?'

'Don't talk about her.'

'Why didn't you go out with her tonight, Tina?'

'Psych. Psych. Psych.' I walked over to him. 'Psych. Psych. Psych.' Getting real close to those eyes of his. 'I know your game, pussy eyes.'

'Yes, it really is all a game, isn't it, Tina? That's why I gave you a home. Because I wanted to play a game. Yes?'

'Piss off.' I walked to the back of the church. 'What are these, pussy eyes?'

'Hymn books.'

I took a few out of the bookcase. Carried them to him. 'Why don't you sing a hymn then, if they're hymn books?'

'What hymn d'you want me to sing?'

'Any hymn. I don't care.' I threw the books at him. Then I sat on one of those wooden chairs. 'Go on, then. I'm listening. Sing a hymn.'

It was real crazy. He picked a hymn and he just

started singing. And I sat there listening to him. But suddenly he looked so weak and vulnerable and soft, and it made me cry. Because I'd been such a pig. Making him sing like that when he was all on his own, with no music or anything. I felt such a pig, it made me cry. His voice, yer see. It sounded so lonely. Terribly lonely. As if no one had ever loved it. No one. Ever.

I don't know what I was doing when I walked towards him. Just a strong feeling that I wanted to touch him. Just touch him. I was scared to touch him, though. He'd stopped singing and when I was inches away from him I just stood there doing nothing.

'Don't leave me.' My voice sounded different. As if it didn't belong to me. 'Don't leave me, will you? No matter what I do.'

'I'm not going anywhere, Tina. I'm here.'

I had the words on my lips then. About Sheena. The frame-up job. Sheena making me do the job. The words were in my mouth. But I remembered her knife. Knew she'd use it.

'Is there something else?' he asked. Taking hold of my hand then. And just holding it. Ever so gently he held it. 'Is there, love?'

I wiped at my runny nose with the back of my hand. Tried to stop the tears from coming. The words, in my mouth. But loyalty. Above it all there had to be loyalty. To her. Sheen. What about loyalty? Could it go to hell?

'You don't have to be scared of telling me anything, Tina. Whatever it is. I'll try my best to help you with it.'

I looked down at his hand. And touched his fingers with my other hand. Very gently I just stroked them.

They were soft. Really soft. He had short nails. Clean nails. Black hairs on his fingers. I didn't think that hand would ever hit me. I just knew it wouldn't. It was too soft. Too soft.

'Don't you want to tell me anything, Tina?'

'I don't know.'

'Are you frightened?'

'Please don't make me tell you anything.' I couldn't grass on Sheena. I just couldn't. Couldn't. She made me so scared.

'I won't make you do anything. Not by force.'

'Dad made me.'

'I know.'

'But you're not like him.'

'No.'

'He never held my hand anyway.'

'It was like an illness he had, Tina.'

'Hate, that's all.'

'Hate is an illness. Of sorts.'

'D'you hate anyone?'

'Not really. I try hard not to, anyway.'

We were silent again then. Silent. But the words were still there. Crammed into my mouth. God. It was a fight. To keep them in or let them out. And we just stayed there, Uncle Howard and me. Uncle Howard, sitting, waiting. He knew there was something else. I could tell he knew.

'Where's Rebecca?' I asked. Just to get the subject on to her. Making my mouth seem emptier. Freer.

'She's down at the pub.'

'Me and Sheen saw her there once.'

'Did you?'

'Yeah. What she does is quite good, isn't it? With the centre. I went in there. It's quite good.'

'She does her best. Sometimes I have to stamp on her a bit, though. Calm her down. She's a bit of a rebel at heart.'

'Is she?'

'She's got a wild streak in her,' he smiled. 'We all try to help her to channel it. And she is coping with it now. Very well, really.'

It made me sick. Gut sick. Hearing that. We're gonna frame her, I wanted to say. We're gonna frame her. Spoil everything.

'Temperaments can be channelled, Tina. Very effectively. God makes everyone different, you see. But everyone's got a purpose. Everyone has. Even you. It's just finding that purpose, isn't it? Using your whole temperament. Your whole being to the full.'

'I'd never be any good at anything.' Except crime. That's what Sheen had said. Except crime.

'That's defeatism, Tina. You can't be a defeatist. You have to have faith in yourself. You're just as good as the next person, you have to believe that. I believe that of you, Tina. And I believe you've got a lot to offer inside you. A lot to offer.'

'We're gonna frame her.' I said it. The words were out in front of me. I pulled away from Uncle Howard. Disgusted with them. Disgusted with myself. But they still came. 'We're gonna frame her,' I yelled. 'Fix her up with drugs. That's what we're going to do. And we're gonna bust up things at the centre. Ruin it all.'

'Tina!'

'Well, that's what you wanted to hear, isn't it? Now you've heard it.' I left the church. Slamming the door. Walked back to the house. Up to my bedroom.

I grabbed my notepad. Wanted to write something but couldn't. I ran the pen across the pad. Hard. So that it tore through a few sheets. I did that again and again.

He didn't knock. He just came straight in the room.

'OK, Tina. I want to hear it all.' Anger sounded. 'Come on.'

'So you want me to get cut up, do yer?'

'Don't shout, just talk.'

'You're shouting.'

'I want you to tell me everything. Now.'

'Just because it's your family. That's all you're worried about.'

'You're going to plant drugs on Rebecca, is that right? So, where're you getting the drugs from?'

'Plant drugs or get cut up. What would you do, then? You know everything. What would you do?'

'You won't get cut up. Not by anyone. That's a promise.'

'What're you going to do then? Fight Sheena? She could cut you in two.'

'I'm not going to fight anyone. I'm just going to get this thing sorted out.'

'Tell me how, then. You can't stop Sheena from doing anything, you know. You can't stop her.'

'I can't but God can.'

'God? Who the hell's God? I don't know him. I'm pissing off out of here anyway. D'yer know I've only got one friend in this lousy world? One friend. And that's my motorbike.' I slammed all the doors in the house on my way out. Kicked open the garden gate and yanked on my crash helmet.

'Hiya, chicken.' Sheen was there. Walking towards me.

I said nothing. Past her. Handled my bike keys.

'Hey!' She came after me. Dancing, sort of. 'Hey, how's Daddy then?'

'Piss off!' I yelled. Pushing her out of the way. Getting on Lobby. Key in ignition.

'No one tells me to piss off, chicken.' Her words combined with the roar of Lobby. I didn't hear any more of them, though, as I rode away.

I turned left outside the vicarage. On to the main road. I clipped my visor down and pushed my bike up through the gears.

As I was approaching the traffic lights I saw her. In my mirror. Behind me. I was scared. Real scared. For a vague second I thought of turning round and heading back to the vicarage. But that thought was quickly gone. I wouldn't have had the time.

The traffic lights were on green. Green, amber, just as I was crossing them. I breathed a sigh of relief. They'd stop her for a couple of minutes. Giving me some headway.

I was so intent on going faster that the sound of the crash didn't really register. It was a crash. I heard the screeching of the brakes. And then the explosion. Metal. But it wasn't important to me. I was just worried about Sheena getting close. Sheena catching me. It was when I looked in my mirror again, and then turned round to find her nowhere in sight, that the thought plummeted through me. The sound of the crash.

I pulled in to the side of the road. Waiting for her.

'Come on,' I was muttering. 'Come on.' In complete contrast to my earlier fear of her. Suddenly. Suddenly everything had changed.

She didn't come.

Then my heart beat fast with a different kind of fear.

A sinking, draining sort of fear. I turned my bike round. Rode back towards the crossroads. The traffic had already begun piling up. I had to ride outside the queue.

The motorbike was in a heap on the middle of the crossing. It was her motorbike. I was numb. Completely numb as I threw my helmet down and walked across to it. People were everywhere, it seemed. People. But there was no sign of Sheen. Hope filled me. She'd walked away from it.

'She went across the red light,' I heard one man say.

Then I saw the lorry. Further down the road. With more people. I walked down there. I don't know why. It was about a hundred yards down the road. Nowhere near Sheen's bike. But I walked slowly towards it. Slowly. Slowly. Slowly. Slowly. Slowly.

She was lying there. Her helmet still on. But she was screaming. Screaming. Then I saw her legs. They weren't with her. They almost looked as if they'd been completely wrenched away from her. They were entangled in the lorry's twisted metal mudguards. Twisted within that and the wheel. Blood was everywhere.

'Help me,' she was screaming. 'Help me, please.'

I just stood there. Doing nothing. For a minute. One. Two. Three. I don't know how long it was, I stood there. But then something snapped within me. Like a stretched elastic band, suddenly giving way.

'Get away from her,' I yelled. 'Leave her alone.' I pushed people out of the way. 'Get the ambulance! What you doing? Get an ambulance.'

'The ambulance is on its way, love.'

'Who are you?' a woman holding Sheen's hand, said. 'Are you a friend?'

'She's my sister. She's my sister. Oh Christ, let me hold her.'

'All right, come round here. Sheena,' she said, wiping Sheena's face with a towel. 'Sheena, here's your sister. Your sister's here.'

'Christ, where's the ambulance? Where's the ambulance? Get it, will yer, get it.'

'Sheen, it's Tina. I'm here.' I held her hand.

'Knock me out, will yer? Knock me out.'

'The ambulance is coming. You'll be OK.'

'My legs. Christ.'

'It's all right. You'll be OK.'

'The lorry. It came out of nowhere.'

I didn't know what to say. She just kept squeezing my hand so tight. Then someone came with a pillow for her and another blanket. Then there were sirens. But it wasn't the ambulance. Police, it was.

'It's the police,' I told Sheena. 'The ambulance will be here soon.'

'Where's Micky?' she said.

'He's coming,' I lied.

'Christ, I'm gonna die. I'm gonna die.'

'No you ain't,' I shouted. 'No you ain't. You've got to fight. Fight.'

She was quieter then. Closed her eyes.

'You ain't gonna die, Sheena.' I tried to instil that fact into her. Trying to convince myself at the same time.

'So much pain,' she muttered.

'Hello, love,' the policeman said to me. Crouching. 'All right, love,' he said to Sheena, stroking her hair. 'The ambulance is just coming. We'll have you away from here in no time.'

'What's happened to my legs?' she said.

'They're fine. Broken, I spect. Won't take long to mend though. Your bike's not too bad. You'll be pleased about that, won't you?'

The ambulance and fire engine came together.

The policeman asked me where our parents lived. And I told him we were staying with Uncle Howard at the vicarage. He took it down in his notepad. Then the ambulance crew came and the firemen, and I had to get out of their way.

'Come and sit down on the kerb, love.' That same woman who'd been comforting Sheena. 'Come on. I've made some coffee, plenty of sugar. It'll do you good.'

I was shivering. Real shivering. Freezing. I sat on the kerb. The woman sat too. Taking my hand and giving me a cup of coffee. That was after she'd wrapped a blanket around my shoulders.

'Is she gonna die?' I asked.

'I don't know, love,' she said. 'You're staying with Howard, aren't you?'

'Yeah.'

'I'm his secretary. Sheena told me your surname and I knew it was you.'

'What's happened to her legs?'

'The lorry was going too fast up to the traffic lights. He knocked her off first and then carried her along.'

'Christ, he must have been doing a ton.'

'He should have slowed down, shouldn't he?'

'I'm going over to her. I've got to be with her.'

'You can't come any closer, love,' the policeman said. 'She's being well looked after now. As soon as we get her free of the lorry you can be with her.'

They'd put her on drips of some sort. Three different sorts. And she was lying still. But her eyes were still open. One of the ambulance men was talking to her.

'What're they doing with that stuff?' The firemen were carrying some sort of equipment.

'They've got to cut the lorry so that they'll be able to free her.'

More sirens. Another ambulance. And a white car with a blue light. Two men in suits got out.

'You're really best sitting down, love,' the policeman said. 'We'll call you as soon as there's enough room.'

I didn't sit down, though. I stayed there, walking slowly around all the activity. That's when I stood by the two men in suits and heard one of them.

'Below the knee,' he said. 'Yeah, we can save the knee.'

'Piss off.' I charged into them. 'You ain't taking her . . .'

'Ssssshhhh!' the man motioned. 'Keep your voice down. We don't want her to hear. Just be quiet and calm down. You're not helping her at all by losing control.'

His words had a sobering effect on me. It was the way he'd spoken.

'We are going to have to take the right leg off. Now. To get her free. It's completely crushed and totally beyond all repair. But with a bit of luck we can save the left one. We're going to put her out now so that she'll know nothing about it. So if you want to sit with her while she's going out, you can do so. But don't get her worked up.'

'Sheen?' I took her hand. Knelt in amongst all the wires surrounding her. 'Sheen, it's Tina. They're gonna make you go to sleep. So you won't be in any more pain. All right?'

'Yeah. Is Mick here?'

'He's just coming.'

'OK.'

'It's all right now, Sheen. You're being well looked after. You got all the cops out, yer know.'

'I never bleeding caught yer.' She actually smiled then.

I smiled too. Crying as well. Crying. At the way she'd smiled.

'I never got the drugs tonight,' she said. 'So, we're clean.'

'Don't worry about nothing, Sheen. Just you, that's all.'

'Reckon I'm gonna sleep now. The pains not too bad. These pissing drips, doing some good.'

'Yeah.'

'Is Uncle Howard here?'

'They've called him.'

'Christ, why don't he hurry? Tell him to come to the hospital and see me, will yer?'

'Don't be stupid. Of course he'll come anyway.'

'Pissing lorry.' That was the last thing she said before she went to sleep. 'Pissing lorry.'

'All right, love? Your uncle's here.'

Chapter 14

We didn't say anything, Uncle Howard and I. I just left Sheena. Walked away from her. Walked away from the lorry. From the flashing fire engine, ambulances and police cars. I left Uncle Howard to be with Sheen. He was with her an hour. All the while it took them to amputate her right leg and to free the other one from the lorry.

I just sat on the kerb. A policeman chatted to me for a while and then left. I sat on the kerb and waited. I was praying, I s'pose. Dear God. The God I don't even know. Dear God. I was praying to him then. Because he, whoever he was, was Sheen's only hope. He. Who I turned to. Then.

Uncle Howard looked awful. He sat on the kerb next to me. White, he looked.

'God, what a mess,' he said, running his hands over his face.

'Is she dead?'

'No. No.'

'Will she die?'

'It's a big shock to her body. If she can cope with that she won't.'

'You said God could stop her from cutting me.'

He laughed. Just slightly. Ironically.

'Yes. I said that.'

'But you didn't mean like this.'

'No, Tina. I didn't mean like this.'

'They're putting her in the ambulance.'

'Yes. Are you going with her? Can you cope with it? She's one hell of a mess.'

'I can cope with it.'

'Good girl. I'll follow in the car.'

'She asked for you to go to the hospital, you know. Just before she went out she asked that.'

'Come on.' He pulled me from the kerb, then cupped my face in his hands. 'Come on. Be strong.' He wiped some of my tears away. 'Be strong, now, when you have to be.'

'I don't want her to die.'

'Neither do I.'

We looked at each other then. His eyes, they were wet with tears. And we understood, we understood perfectly what the other was going through. We understood. Because we both felt the same. I knew we did.

I walked towards the ambulance. They were moving her on to a stretcher. It was awful. Her leg. Her thigh was sticking up in the air, hopelessly lost. Meat. It just looked like a piece of meat. Hospital equipment was being pushed next to her stretcher. I got in the ambulance and sat there. Watching them bring her in. Her other leg was completely twisted. Her toes touching her leg, her heel completely severed.

The ambulance men and the doctors were talking but they all seemed a long way away to me. Just Sheena's face I saw. Completely untouched by the accident. Her unblemished skin as white as the pillow she was resting on. But then the wires. Up her nose. Down her throat.

'Leave her alone,' I wanted to scream. 'Leave her

alone. She's mine. She's mine. She's mine. All mine.'

The ambulance couldn't travel all that fast because she was so ill. Then, at one stage, they were worried because her pulse seemed to be dropping. So they injected some stuff into her and she was OK again.

I felt relieved to reach the hospital, though. It was so comforting to see the group of white-coated doctors and uniformed nurses waiting for us. It was so comforting to see how they quickly, efficiently rushed her away.

And then Uncle Howard was there. Leading me into the small waiting-room. Then a nurse came to see us.

'There really isn't much more you can do here,' she said. 'They'll be a few hours in the theatre. Why don't you go home and get some rest? We'll ring you as soon as we hear.'

'It's all right. We'll wait until after the operation. I'd like to see a doctor as soon as I can,' Uncle Howard said.

'All right. I'll bring you both a cup of tea.'

I lit a fag. Closed my eyes. Wondered what was happening. Wondered if it was all real. I looked at Uncle Howard. The dimple on his chin. His hands resting on his lap. Then he looked at me and smiled. 'She'll make it,' he said.

'D'you know?' God might have told him.

'Well, she never gives up, does she? Always wins her fights.'

'Yeah.'

He held my hand then.

'She was coming after me, you know,' I said.

'Was she?'

'Chasing me. I met her when I went out of the house. I told her to piss off. Then I went off on my bike and she came after me. When I went through the traffic lights they were green, just turning to amber.'

'And she went through them when they were red.'

'We used to be always doing that. And Micky. Shooting the lights. Crazy, isn't it?'

'Yes. Just a bit.'

'Excitement. That's all it was for.'

'I know. You're all in search of excitement.'

'It was my fault. If I hadn't told her to piss off she wouldn't have come after me.'

'It was no one's fault. Don't blame yourself. It won't do her any good, will it? Or you.'

'It won't do her any good. Not now.'

Not now.

Not now.

The nurse brought us some tea. Then about ten minutes after, the doctor came and took Uncle Howard away. I waited with a few other people. I wondered why they were waiting. What they were waiting for.

What?

The time ticked on.

Uncle Howard came back.

'They're going to try and save her left leg,' he said. 'They said she's very strong and should come through but they're not sure about her leg. They're not sure.' He sat down. Sighing.

I didn't know whether to feel relieved they said she was strong or not. Could I take it for a certainty that she was going to survive? And what if she did? It was gradually sinking into me then. The sight of her thigh, grotesquely sticking in the air. Nothing attached. They're going to try and save her left leg. Try. Try.

'Christ!' I said. 'No legs.'

'She's a fighter.' That's all Uncle Howard said. 'She's a fighter.'

'God.' She'd always had to be.

'I've got to go and ring Rebecca to tell her what's been happening, Tina. All right?'

'OK.'

He rang Becky.

Came back.

We sat. Together. Waiting. Silent.

At two-fifteen in the morning the doctor came back. Called Uncle Howard away again. I was kind of numb. Tired. I don't know. Expecting the worst, I s'pose. She hasn't made it. She's dead. She's gone. She's gone. She's gone.

When Uncle Howard came back he beckoned me to follow him into the corridor.

'She survived the operation,' he said. But I felt nothing. Nothing. 'She's survived but is very weak now. They're doing all they can.'

'What about her other leg?'

'It's OK, Tina. A bit of a mess but OK.'

'I wanna see her.'

'We can't see her yet. She's still in the recovery room. She'll be moved into intensive care tomorrow morning. We can see her then. If she takes a turn for the worse before then we'll be called in.'

I shrugged. What else was there?

'Come on, let's go home.'

It was real awful just leaving her. I felt as if I was betraying her, somehow, by going. Betraying her. But hadn't I done that already? By telling Uncle Howard about her framing Rebecca. But, anyway, did it matter any more? The frame-up job seemed so far away. My fear of her seemed so far away. Our own life, our own years together, they didn't seem to matter any more. Because Sheen had suddenly been torn apart. Her whole existence. Her whole being. Torn apart. Cruelly. Callously.

Chapter 15

'What's so special about your God now, then?' I yelled at Uncle Howard. At nine the next morning. Saturday morning. After I'd had a bad night. 'What's so special about your damned God now?' It was over breakfast. It had annoyed me because when I came down Uncle Howard wasn't around. Daniel told me he'd gone to the church to pray for Sheen. Christ, that really strung me out. So I was ready for him when he came back.

Uncle Howard didn't answer me. Just buttered a piece of toast which Jilly had done for him.

'You can't tell me, can you? Because he ain't special, is he? And if he's there all he does is piss on everyone.'

'I don't want that language at the breakfast table.'

'Sometimes what you want you can't have. Or has no one ever told you that?'

'Why don't you stop shouting at Dad?' Daniel suddenly started shouting. 'He hasn't slept all night. He's been up ringing the hospital every two hours. And you're not the only one who cares about Sheena round here, you know. Why don't you just think of someone else for a change?' He walked out of the back door then. Slamming it after him.

I said nothing. Tension was around us like electricity.

'D'you want some more toast, Jilly?' Rebecca asked.

'Yes please. One more bit.'

'D'you want some toast, Tina?'

'No thanks.'

'You haven't eaten anything, Tina,' she said. 'You should have something. It'll make you feel better.'

'I don't feel like anything.'

'Try, Tina,' Uncle Howard said.

'I said I didn't want anything, OK?' I shouted.

'All right, don't bloody have anything,' he yelled. 'Just don't answer me back any more today. I've had enough.'

It stung me. The way he shouted. Just a bit, it stung me.

'Do people always shout when someone's in hospital?' Jilly asked.

'Get up to your room, Jilly,' he yelled again. Standing then. 'And stay there until I tell you otherwise.'

'Why? What've I done?' Her face broke and tears started to come.

'You know what you've done. Just get upstairs.'

'Dad!' Rebecca intervened. 'She didn't mean anything.'

'I'm well aware of what her tone of voice meant. Now, get upstairs. And don't you dare slam any doors. I'm sick of slammed doors round here.'

Jilly went. Quietly.

'That was unfair, Dad,' Rebecca said.

He didn't answer.

I went over to the hospital on my motorbike. I didn't fancy going with Uncle Howard.

When I got there I was shown where the intensive care unit was. Sheen was in the unit in a cubicle of her own. Loads of machinery around her. Wires coming from every part of her, it seemed. She was awake. You know, it was good to see her awake. I thought she'd be asleep.

She smiled at me.

'Hi,' I said. Keeping my eyes away from the bed. Away from where the outline of her leg should have been. 'You OK?'

'Sit down. There's a chair.'

'I can't stay long. The nurse said ten minutes.'

'Ten minutes. If I stay awake that long.'

'Uncle Howard's coming later. This afternoon.'

'What about Micky?'

'Uncle Howard's contacting him today.'

'Yer know they've cut me leg off?'

'Yeah. I know.'

'Look then. Just look at the bed.'

I looked.

'I can still feel the bastard.'

I smiled. At her swearing.

'I thought you'd bleeding had it.'

'Me? They didn't think I'd be awake today. The doc. calls me his fighting girl. Me? Die? No chance. I ain't ready yet. Not to die.'

She closed her eyes then. For a few minutes. I just sat there, watching her. Different. So different she looked. I couldn't believe what I was seeing. It was crazy.

'Hey.' She opened her eyes. 'You're dreaming again.'

'Yeah.'

'Dreamer. You and your notepad.'

'What?'

'I've been reading it for years. You can't keep nothing from me.'

'Bitch.' I smiled.

'Good stories. Dreams. Good dreams.'

I started crying then.

'Don't blub.'

'You're just taking it so well.'

'Yeah. But what else is there? I can't give up. I ain't giving up. That's why I'm talking to yer now. 'Cos I never gave up.'

'You never did give up on a fight.'

'Tearaway.'

'Yeah.'

'Not with one leg.'

'A wooden foot would hurt more.'

She smiled then.

'It's over, Tina.'

'What?'

'Me. What I was. We lost a leg, for Christ's sake.' She reached for my hand then. Tears ran down her face.

'You'll be OK,' I assured her. Determined that she would be. 'I'll make sure of that.'

'Anyway, Uncle Howard ain't gonna chuck us out, is he?'

'Of course not.'

'Crazy bastard. Taking us in first of all.'

'Yeah.'

'Some vicar.'

'Pussy eyes.'

'You told him, didn't yer? About the frame-up job.'

I nodded.

'But I had to fight them, Teens. I had to fight them.' As if she was giving me an explanation.

'I know yer did.'

'But now I'll give in gracefully.'

'It won't be easy. It's not easy. You always feel like fighting them. Always.'

'I'll be too busy fighting to walk.'

'Yeah.'

'And you'll be too busy doing whatever you're going to be doing.'

'Not much.'

'Rebecca needs some help in the church.'

'What?'

'She wants to change things. Make church more relaxed. So more people would go. She's in a fight with Uncle Howard, though. He wants things to stay as they are.'

'Uncle Howard said she's a real rebel.'

'And she needs more support to change things. To let more people into the circle, baby. I've seen plenty of rebels, but she's a rebel with a cause and that's different. She's special. Stick in with her, Tina.'

'Fight Uncle Howard?'

'Butter him up. He's all right. Just too stubborn. I know he's stubborn. Because things went on between us two, as well. Little things. I wasn't winning all the time.'

'Weren't yer?'

'He was too determined.'

We both laughed then.

'Hey,' she said.

'Yeah.'

'Make me a promise.'

'What?'

'Don't get on yer bike again. Tell Rebecca to give up hers. I'll tell her too. I don't want neither of you to get back on them again. It ain't worth it, Tina. Too dangerous.'

'I rode it over here.'

'Ride it back. That's all. Promise me, Tina. Please.'

'OK, I promise.'

'Thanks.'

The nurse came in then. 'I've given you a few minutes extra,' she said. 'But no more.'

'OK, fatso.' Sheen smiled. 'But I ain't tired. I can go more than ten minutes.'

'D'you see what I have to put up with?' The nurse turned to me.

'Until you move me out of intensive care. I'm strong, aren't I? Fit. Healthy.'

'You'll be healthy if the doctor finds out you've been going over your time.'

'OK, you win. You've got the doctor on your side, I know. I bet you and him are secret lovers, yer know?'

'He's married, actually.'

'That stops yer?'

'I'll be going then, Sheen,' I butted in to their back-chat.

'OK. Thanks for coming.'

'See yer then, Sheen.'

'And Uncle Howard's coming this afternoon.'

'Yeah.'

'Tell him not to come in his bleeding dog-collar. It'll make me feel like I'm dying.'

'OK, I'll tell him. Bye, then.' I kissed her.

'Bye – and hey!'

'What?'

'You're meant to bring people presents when they're in hospital.'

'Piss off! I never thought you'd be alive to give you bleeding presents.'

'Language!' the nurse said as I was going out. 'Language.' In a nice sort of way she said it.

Chapter 16

We were eating lunch when there was a ring at the door.

'I'll go.' Jilly jumped up and ran out. 'It's your brother, Tina. It's Tina's brother, Dad.'

I rushed out. Feeling really glad that he'd come so soon. I was just about to hug him, when he suddenly let fly at me. I went down like a kicked chair, mainly out of surprise, though. Then he yanked me up.

'What did I tell yer?' he bellowed. 'What did I tell yer?' He shook me. So violently, it hurt my neck. Then he shoved me against the wall. 'I told yer to take this chance, didn't I? Didn't I?'

'Piss off! Leave me alone.'

But he kept hitting me.

'So what the hell happened? What were you doing? Trouble again, was it? Trouble. Was it?'

'No. Honest, Micky. Honest. Uncle Howard!'

'Will you please leave Tina alone, Micky. She's in the middle of her lunch.'

'I'm sorry to disturb your lunch. We'll go outside.'

'Just leave her alone. You've got the wrong end of the stick. Tina's been no trouble here at all. A few ups and downs but nothing serious. It was an accident. A bad accident. No one's to blame, Micky.'

'Yeah, well, I appreciate what you're saying but just in case there was anything else involved I'm gonna give her one.'

'I think you've given her one already. And it's not

going to solve anything, is it? Sheena's still in hospital with one leg.'

'Yeah, that's right. And someone's got to answer for that, haven't they? I thought I told you to keep her straight,' he yelled at me again.

'I couldn't,' I screamed. 'It was too hard. You don't know. You've never gone straight, have you?'

'I'm gonna make sure you never get the chance to do anything else but go straight.' He began to unbuckle his belt.

'You ain't touching me with that belt. You bastard.'

'You take that belt off and I'll get the police in here,' Uncle Howard said.

'Leave the police out of it,' I yelled. 'Just stop him hitting me.'

Micky had taken his belt off and was dragging me to the door. I never saw Rebecca. Not until she was suddenly there. And the next minute there was Micky sprawled on the floor. And Rebecca standing there with a milk bottle in her hand.

I looked at her.

Uncle Howard looked first at Micky and then at Rebecca. In utter astonishment.

Rebecca shrugged.

'Well, thank you very much,' Uncle Howard said. 'You dealt with the situation very effectively.' Sarcastic he was being.

'Well, you weren't doing anything,' she answered.

'I was just going to call the police.'

'We don't want them in here, Dad.'

He stared at her then. Real cross, like. But she didn't care.

'Let's get him in and close the door,' she said. Beginning to drag Micky.

'What's happening, Dad?'

'Go back in the lounge, Jilly.'

'Who hit him?' Daniel joined her. 'Becky, did you hit him?'

'Yes, darling.'

'Wow.'

'It's nothing to be proud of, Daniel,' Uncle Howard interjected.

'Did Becky save Tina?' Jilly asked.

'Yeah.' Daniel. 'I'll help.'

So Rebecca, Daniel and me dragged Micky in and shut the front door.

'Yuk. He's bleeding.' Jilly peered at his head.

'Go in the lounge, Jilly and Daniel.' Uncle Howard pushed both of them towards the lounge door. 'Is he bleeding badly, Becky?'

'No, Dad. It's only a cut.'

'I don't want blood all over the carpet.'

'Dad!'

But then Micky started stirring. All three of us just watched him. Watched him slowly come round. Sit up. With his head in his hands.

'Are you all right?' Uncle Howard asked.

'What hit me?'

'I hit you with a milk bottle,' Rebecca said, putting a wet cloth on his head where the cut was.

'Thanks, love,' he said.

'You were going to hit Tina, that's why.'

'Oh yeah, I remember.'

'We don't want any hitting round here. We're a happy family.' She smiled at Uncle Howard when she said that. But he didn't smile back.

'So you won't hit her, will you? You really just needed calming down. You're upset about Sheen, we know. But hitting Tina isn't going to do any good. It wasn't her fault.'

'What happened then? Just tell me what happened.'

'She went through a red light,' I said. 'She was chasing me. She went through a red light.'

'Chasing yer?'

'Yeah. I told yer it was hard. We had arguments. So, she chased me. That's all. She went through a red light. You always go through red lights.'

He shook his head. 'Crazy bitch.'

'She's OK, Micky. She's accepted it. Go and see her.'

He got to his feet. Slowly. Howard brought him a chair. He sat down.

'I'll make you a cup of tea.' Uncle Howard went into the kitchen.

'You're not going to hit her any more, are you, Micky?' Rebecca asked.

'No, love.' Micky smiled at her.

'OK.' And she went back into the lounge, taking Daniel and Jilly with her.

Micky looked at me.

'Sorry, Micky. I couldn't keep her straight because it's hard for me being here too.'

'All right. I know. But now what's going to happen?'

'Uncle Howard says he'll still give us a home.'

'D'you want to stay?'

'Of course.'

Micky sighed. 'Well, if you do stay I've decided to give myself up, make a clean slate. I'm sick of running.'

'It won't be easy. And you haven't got anyone like Uncle Howard either.'

'Just to see you two on the straight and narrow will inspire me. I hope. I hope.'

He hoped. Like I once hoped.

'Tea's ready in the kitchen,' Uncle Howard said.

'Dad, we'll have to put all the dinners in the oven again to warm up.' Jilly came out.

'All right, we'll do that,' Uncle Howard smiled.

All right.

'We'll do that, love.' Uncle Howard ruffled her hair. 'We'll do that.'

Amen.